The Bridge to Tybee

Thomas J. Murphy

Old Fort Press
Savannah, Georgia

The Bridge to Tybee

Library of Congress Control Number: 2025901846

This book is a work of fiction. Names, characters, places, and events either are the product of the author's imagination or used fictitiously.

ISBN: 978-1-964278-03-2 (Paperback)

ISBN: 978-1-964278-04-9 (E-book)

In Memory of
My Mother and Father
"True to the Last"

Requiescat in Pace

Foreword

By Father Brett Brannen

I am honored to write the foreward for this intriguing novel, filled with so many things which compose the days of our lives: things like growing up, coming of age, love, family, faith, education, friendships, war, pain, heroism, and death. I have known Fr. Thomas J. Murphy for 40 years. We were in the same seminary at the same time. I knew his wonderful, faith-filled parents and his dear sisters. I lived with him in the same rectory at St. Joseph's in Macon, Ga. He was very kind to me when I was young, "in the business," so to speak, and always there for me as a good friend. I am humbled to write the foreward for this book. However, as the current pastor of St. Michael Catholic Church on Tybee Island, I feel somewhat qualified, even compelled, to write it.

Fr. Murphy is a laid-back, honest, holy, and humble priest. He is also a realist! He understands that people struggle in life, and he is always present to listen, walk with them in their pain, and pray with and for them. His own sufferings have taught him to love people like the Master loves, with mercy and patience. This book is the fruit of his over 40 years of priestly ministry.

I was given a copy of this manuscript about five years ago. I was surprised, as I had not even known he was writing a book! Later, I learned that he had written much of it on his cell phone while sitting on a bench at the beach on Tybee Island! After I read it, I advised him: "This is excellent. Publish it immediately!"

Tybee Island (aka Savannah Beach) is a beloved place to old Savannah families. For a southern city, Savannah has a lot of Irish Catholic influence. The Murphys were one of these hard-working, respectable, faithful Catholic families. You will see the expressions and traditions, the attitude towards life, family, faith, and fun come and go like the tide in these pages. The book is written "in a time" shortly after "The Marsh Hen" ceased to run, and the road to Tybee was built. Before the road, the railroad or a boat were the only ways to get to Tybee! The train was aptly named. My grandmother told me stories of getting on The Marsh Hen after church on Sunday and going out to Tybee for the day. The last train left at 5:00 p.m. and you better be on it, if you did not want to sleep on the beach!

The Bridge to Tybee is a novel that describes what we all come to know as we grow in age, grace, and wisdom: Life Happens. We grow up. We make our choices. Some are good, and some are bad. We all have our joys and sorrows, our successes and failures, our pleasures and our pains. But as the novel concludes, we are reminded of the truth that life is good. God is good! He loves us and wants us to be eternally happy with him in Heaven. Fr. Murphy's deep but gentle faith is hidden on every page.

I attended an awards ceremony here in Savannah about ten years ago, The St. Thomas More Society; Catholic Lawyer of the Year. The recipient was very elderly and distinguished. He was from "the old guard". He received the award and then told us this poem he had written:

> "If I die and go to Heaven, this is how I'll know. I'll find myself on Tybee, forty years ago."
> *Ed Brennan*

Tolle et Lege. Take and read! The Bridge to Tybee is a book you will continue to ponder even after completion.

Fr. Brett Brannen
>   Pastor St. Michael Catholic Church
>   Tybee Island, Ga.
>   Vicar for Priestly Life and Vocations
>   Catholic Diocese of Savannah
>   Author of "To Save a Thousand Souls: A Guide for Discerning a Vocation to Diocesan Priesthood (2010) and "A Priest in the Family: A Guide for Parents Whose Sons Are Considering Priesthood (2014)

THE BRIDGE TO TYBEE

THOMAS J. MURPHY

Chapter 1

The Lot

The old man gazes out the window at the marsh, his thoughts drifting more to the past than the present. He sits low in the passenger seat, his fingers idly playing with a floppy light blue hat. Henry McGee had called his son, Philip, to take him to the Savannah Beach. Tybee has its own identity, but it is still called "The Beach" by Savannahians and so many others who flock to her during the season between May and September. Philip glances over at his dad. "I think the Atlantic wants the roadbed back, Dad. It covers it at high tide."

They drive along for a while, both lost in thought, until Philip breaks the silence. "You've always said that going to Tybee is like leaving Savannah without leaving Savannah. I think I finally understand that now."

Henry glances at his son and smiles, then notices where they are on their journey. They pass a public boat ramp on the right, and Phil notices a pickup truck pulling a boat trailer holding a little skiff getting ready to launch it into the tidal creek.

"This was part of the old road to Tybee, Phil. Some old

timers like me used to call it Shell Road," Henry explains. "It's still lined with those old palm trees planted in memory of Georgia soldiers killed in the Great War. And up ahead, there once stood the old Lazaretto Creek Bridge. Phil Keane, your namesake, called it 'The Bridge to Everywhere or the Bridge to Nowhere.' I remember crossing it in my old DeSoto like it was yesterday. It was an old draw bridge with silver-colored trestles straight across the creek to Tybee. I never lived at Tybee, though, except for two months in the Summer of 1947."

Phil McGee gets back onto the "new highway." He crosses the present Lazaretto Creek Bridge, which offers a picturesque view of the Lazaretto Creek flowing into the Atlantic Ocean and the north and south river channels meeting these waters and emptying into and out of the Atlantic Ocean.

On the left is the historic Cockspur Island Lighthouse, surrounded by water as the tide rushes in. Several container ships enter the north channel stacked to the gills, delivering all sorts of merchandise from Europe and the East to the Port of Savannah. The huge container ships appear as ghost ships coming out of the morning mist and then as WWII aircraft carriers as they come closer to the channel. Instead of carrying Bell and Boeing-built fighter planes, these ships are loaded with multicolored stacks of rectangular-shaped containers seven high—yellow, green, orange, blue, and even pink.

The father and son drive over a small bridge over a tidal creek.

"Take a right up here at the caution light," Henry orders.

Phil turns his Honda down a side street that runs along the marsh and little tidal creek on the backside of the Island. A few empty lots exist, but most homes are built off the ground.

"Now drive slow," Henry says. "Slow, Phil,..." he says again. "OK...here...stop here." Henry signals with his right hand. "There it is, the hammock or the "Lot" as we used to call it," he says.

Dad had never shown him the "Lot" before, but he's been talking about it lately. "Kind of a small island, Dad," Phil remarks.

"That's what a hammock is, son, a very small island in the marsh. Now let me put my legs out of the car and sit a moment," the old man says.

"Let me just sit a little while," he says again.

"Peg O' My Heart," he whispers.

"Mom?" Phil asks.

"Your mother, Phil, Margaret Conner McGee, Peg O' My Heart," Henry McGee whispers.

The old man stares at the little island. His eyes glaze over, deep in thought. "I remember it like it was yesterday," he says in a whisper.

And in that instant, it was.

Chapter 2

The Old Neighborhood
1947

Henry McGee walks out of his small one-story white wooden house onto the screened porch as Tina, the lady who helps his mother, hollers at him from inside.

"Henry, you going to Tybee again? You know your momma needs you around the house...and now you're going down there to do God knows what?!"

Henry smiles and answers, "That's why Mother has you, Tina!"

"Boy, let me tell you something, ain't no one...butler, maid, chauffeur, or whoever, ever gonna replace a son. Now go on and get and be careful down there," Tina says from the dark inside of the house, which has all its curtains and blinds drawn to keep out the summer heat. "Lots of trouble on that little island this time of year," she adds.

"Yeah, beer, burgers, crabs, and the big band sound," the twenty-year-old tall, lean, brown-haired, fair-skinned vet wearing a dark blue T-shirt, long khaki pants, and black high-top sneakers mutters to himself, smiling. "It's Tybee time," he whispers.

As he walks down the few steps from the porch in front of his house, Henry glances across the street and remembers watching his brother Karl swing from the old tire tied by a thick rope onto a large branch gloriously growing out of a grand oak. The old tire and rope would swing over the empty lot on Lincoln Street, with Karl holding onto it like a life raft while smiling and yelling.

As a small child, under the watchful eye of his mother and the family maid, Henry would look over from the porch because he was not allowed to run around the neighborhood yet. As a toddler just learning to walk, Henry longed to join Karl. He would watch Karl and the older boys swing and play on the crudely fashioned see-saw. Up and down they'd go, and looking back to those days, it seemed the swing swung further, and the see-sawers soared higher. Later, Henry would join them in games of half rubber in the street and basketball in front of the hoop-and-backboard nailed roughly ten feet off the ground onto another old tree.

Henry thought the oak tree Karl swung from must be the oldest in the city, but then he found another one near the old Candler Hospital on Drayton and Gaston. He imagined Yamacraw Indians resting underneath it as they hunted wild game or early settlers resting there as they surveyed the city's outskirts. Oddly enough, he had found an Indian arrowhead nearby as a boy. The arrowhead was made of what he thought to be limestone, certainly imported from further north by the Indian trading system down the old Indian trails, which at one time had run all over Creek and Cherokee territory in what is now Georgia. The branches on the live oak tree and the Spanish moss-covered canopy kept the houses and street shaded and slightly cooler in the dog days of summer.

Henry McGee gets into his 1940 black four-door Chrysler DeSoto with the coach doors. It is parked on Maupas Avenue in a white single-car wood garage. He recently bought the eight-year-old car which was in pretty good shape—not new, but not a jalopy.

His dad inspected the car and observed, "The 6-cylinder motor runs strong and smooth and still has most of its original 55 horsepower. The interior has wear and tear and is a little ratty, but as long as it's 'mechanically sound, the interior doesn't matter. It also has an old car smell, but overall, it's a good car. An automobile is simply to get you from point A to point B."

Henry brakes as he backs out of the short driveway. The brakes squeak and need to be checked. He must wait for the milk wagon traveling back to Annette's Dairy, east down Maupas Avenue towards Habersham.

"Cloppity clop, cloppity clop." The horses' hooves hit the street as they slowly moved past the McGee residence. As a kid, he thought those horses were ten feet high.

The draft horses sweat profusely in the morning heat of late summer. Droplets of perspiration fall from their heads and back, landing on the asphalt, causing little puffs of steam that evaporate quickly. The beasts of burden, with their coachman and delivery man, make their rounds, delivering milk to young people and working mothers and fathers.

Hope they give them plenty of fresh water and hose them down later, especially in this heat. The young man feels empathy for the workhorses.

After the milk wagon passes, Henry turns north onto Lincoln towards Gaston to pick up Jack Butler, a high school classmate and WWII Navy vet. The hottest part of summer is over, as it is late August, but more is coming. Farther north, they call it Indian Summer. Henry remembers that from meeting people from Maryland when he was stationed there with the Navy near the end of WWII.

He and Jack Butler were assigned to Solomon's Island—not

the one in the Pacific where there was actual fighting, but the one in southern Maryland. They had fun writing to classmates and friends from Savannah, telling them they were in "the Solomons." Technically, they were part of the Atlantic Theater and even got a ribbon, and they all got the Victory Medal for serving. They were trained to be skippers of landing craft and were going to be in the invasion of Japan until the A-bomb was dropped, which spared them and thousands of others, if not the people of Hiroshima and Nagasaki.

Jack is the oldest of five boys, tall, slender, fair-skinned, and blue-eyed like Henry. They are both going to the local college but have taken part of the summer quarter off to do odd jobs around town and build a small house on a lot they bought "at the beach." They are going to school thanks to the GI Bill, which provides a temporary $50-plus monthly check from the government for their honorable service and to assist them accordingly.

Chapter 3

Picking up the Guys

Henry blows the horn, and Jack comes running out of his residence, a large Victorian two-story house that needs a paint job. It's divided into four apartments, housing four families. Two of Jack's brothers, who look just like him, stand outside with baseball gloves, tossing a baseball in shorts and T-shirts. Jack is dressed in khakis and a white T-shirt and is holding his white sailor's cap, which unfolds. He'll use it later to protect his face from the Tybee sun. He is wearing black sneakers, as well.

"Don't spend your whole check on beer and dames, Jack!" one of his brothers shouts.

"Don't worry, I will," Jack responds.

"Hey, Henry, Jack will be bumming money off of you by tomorrow!" the other brother yells.

"Neither a lender nor a borrower be," Henry mutters to himself within ear range of Jack's brothers.

"Tell Jack that, Henry," one brother responds as he catches a baseball with his well-worn leather baseball glove. "You knuckleheads, take it easy."

"That's the plan, brother, that's the plan," Jack responds.

Turning to Henry, Jack said, "My brothers are jealous of the check. They wished they'd been old enough to serve." He paused and added, "Speaking of brothers, how's Karl?"

Henry rubbed his hand down his face. "After serving four years in the Pacific, he's a captain and decorated war hero. He was in all the landings with the Corps of Engineers. Was in the thick of it on Leyte Island. He's been sent away for evaluation, 'shell-shocked,' they say. He keeps waking up in cold sweats after nightmares. If he passes everything, he's going to stay in. But I'm worried about him, Jack."

"Man, he is a hero or else a nut," Jack says.

"Watch what you say. That's my brother, Jack," Henry adds.

"Sorry, Henry. I'd say Karl is a hero. Commissioned at nineteen. That's something. He could retire a general if he stays in long enough," Jack adds thoughtfully.

"Yeah, but I don't want him going to war again," Henry says. "Mother and Dad couldn't handle it."

"Forget all that, Henry. Karl's going to be fine. Let's pick up Lafayette and Billy and get to Tybee," Jack says.

The two young men pick up Lafayette Adams, a tall, muscular young man. Then, they retrieve Billy Burns, a short and stocky fellow, at their Savannah eastside homes and head east on Victory, US Highway 80, which runs from Tybee west all the way to San Diego. It had been completed not long before and extended over rivers and marshland to the isolated island, which at one time was only accessible by rail built on a palm-lined railroad bed. The train from President Street to Tybee had been called the "Marsh Hen." It had stopped running about fifteen years prior.

During Prohibition, when Internal Revenue officers were seen getting on the Marsh Hen to Tybee, word was sent ahead to raise the bridge at Lazaretto Creek to give the speakeasies time to quit serving beer and liquor and become legitimate places of business again. Sometimes, it is said the engineer even sounded the steam whistle at Lazaretto Creek to warn of the impending inspections. "The tax man cometh," as the saying goes.

"Henry, stop off at Duane's store and get a case of Pabst. They're fifty cents each," Lafayette says.

If Henry and Jack are the brains, Lafayette Adams is the brawn—older, rougher, and commanding. Billy Burns is the comedian.

"Daggumit, I had to buy Grandpa Burns medicine for his hemorrhoids and groceries for Mom and Dad and my brothers and sisters with my check," Billy says. "I've got thirty-five cents left for the weekend. I'll just drink three bottles of beer."

"Two," Jack says.

"Two and a half," Billy argues.

"How 'bout none, Billy," Lafayette says.

"Oh hell, Lafayette, he can have two of mine," Henry says.

Lafayette pretends to open the "coach doors" on the old DeSoto, asking, "Do you know why they call these doors 'suicide doors,' Burns? Because if you open them while you're driving, the wind will suck you right out onto the roadway." He pretends to open the car door.

"Henry and Butler would testify against you," Billy says.

Billy could have been shell-shocked as he got called up early his senior year and joined the Marines. He was in the Battle of Okinawa and had to use a flamethrower. Billy's only story about that time was when his platoon leader asked him to torch a hole, and he commented, "There might be women and children in there, Lieutenant." The young officer looked at him sternly and asked, "Do you want to go in and see?"

Billy said he turned the torch on, and it lit up the whole tunnel, shooting out of little holes. He said he didn't hear any screams—just grenades exploding and some gunshots. He hoped it was just soldiers, but he couldn't be 100% positive.

Billy had taken a job driving the trash truck when he first came home from the war, but he had been teased by a class-mate. "Another BC Cadet done well!" the boy had said, laughing at him. Billy had gone looking for a new job that after-noon and found one driving the gas truck. He said he didn't like the smell of gasoline, but it paid, and there was an opportunity, especially since Billy likes to drink lots of beer.

The old DeSoto heads east down Victory Drive and passes Daffin Park, where Henry McGee almost drowned swimming in the man-made lake in the shape of the continental U.S. Henry almost drowned in Texas, according to the approximate location on the lake. He and others would dive under the plank bridge built to the little island in the lake and come up for air under the bridge. This time, there was no room due to the higher level of the lake from a few days of rain. Henry still didn't know how he made it back from underneath that bridge. His mother's prayers, he figures.

Mary St. John McGee, named after a nun, lit a little red votive candle daily for "her boys." She had two stars in her window in honor of her two sons, Karl and Henry, off to war. Both Karl and Henry said there were times they felt her prayers. Karl especially, who was clearing off wreckage from a landing strip on Leyte Island during the great battle when a Japanese Zero fired on him while he was manning a bulldoz-er. Suddenly, the Zero turned right and spun out of control, crashing into the jungle ahead of him. A gunner had rifled it with 50 caliber bullets, and the bullets coming from the Zero towards him instead fired towards where the plane ended up going down and exploding. Later, Karl and some buddies cut a piece of metal from the red Zero insignia on one of its wings. Karl gave Henry a small strip of it that Henry kept in a jewelry box.

"That Zero was built with all the old scrap we sent to Japan in the 1930s. Scrap from old DeSoto's brother," he'd tell Henry.

"Well, they didn't get mine!" Henry would respond.

When Karl told his mother about the close call after the war, Mary St. John asked him, "Did you pray for that pilot's soul?"

Karl responded, "Huh?"

His mother said, "That boy had a mother, too, Karl."

Karl still talks about that and says he recently prayed for that Japanese pilot and the pilot's mother at the base chapel. He was beginning to gain a mature understanding of war.

Same way with Henry. He didn't have his older brother's experiences during the war, but he felt his mother's prayers that day under the bridge in "Texas." Since then, he has been more careful about unnecessary risks. He gained a certain wisdom from that experience on the lake. Besides, he didn't want to drown in "Texas" anyway.

The boys ride by Red Donaldson's Johnny Harris Barbecue Restaurant, home of Johnny Harris' Famous Barbecue Sauce, and Victory Drive-In Theater. Henry was "arrested" as a young boy after a fire broke out behind the theater. The police nabbed him and took him straight home to his father, who proceeded to exact the proper punishment of the day—the leather razor strap! He never would use a straight-edge razor, not after that beating.

"I prefer the standard military issue Gillette safety razor myself," Henry would tell his father, who said the straight razor gave a better shave.

Billy remarks that they are driving on part of the same route that the Great Savannah Races were held on about forty years ago, when racers from all over the world came to compete for the Vanderbilt Cup.

"Ain't nothin' left of the track now," Lafayette says.

"Don't matter. They were here, Lafayette. Just like your namesake—the Marquis de Lafayette. He was here, too," Billy responds.

"Yeah, but the porch he stood on when he came to Savannah is the only thing still there. No stands are left, and the track's been paved over," Lafayette responded.

"Still don't matter. Lafayette was here, and so were the Great Savannah Races," Billy states. "Besides, that old farm-house on the left we just passed was where my pop, as a boy, stood on the porch and waived to the racers as they came by. So, stuff is still here."

"Yeah, right, Billy," Lafayette responds.

The old DeSoto crosses Skidaway, and Billy says, "The racers turned their cars right here and raced south. And on the left is St. Mary's Orphanage, where I played Santa Claus for the orphans last Christmas."

"Now that I believe, Billy!" Laf remarks.

"I hope to do it every year. Figure I have penance to do for torching...," Billy stops.

"Let it go, Billy, they'd have 'done you' had you not 'done them,'" Laf says, attempting to comfort his buddy. "Those Nazis got theirs at that Nuremberg place. We were fighting fascists in the Pacific too, and they got theirs, Billy," Laf continues. "Fascists, all fascists."

As the boys approach Thunderbolt, just outside Savannah on Victory, Henry turns the DeSoto into Duane's Groceries for a case of Pabst and a few other supplies. The grocery store sells a little bit of everything. Beer, cigarettes, milk and bread, cold cuts, soda, ice, candy, and boiled peanuts. Also, beach supplies like flip flops, sand buckets, and shovels for the kids. There is lots of stuff outside the grocery store that looks like a little filling station with its small interior and overhang with a pump and Pure Gas sign. There is a big drum filled with bamboo fishing poles and a produce stand with fresh fruit and vegetables like oranges, grapefruit, corn, and black-eyed peas.

Several old men sit out front in chairs, playing checkers, wearing straw hats, smoking pipes, and hand-rolling cigarettes.

The boys address them, "Hello, sirs!"

"Hello, young fellas. Heading to the beach, are ya?" one old fellow asks.

"Yes, sir," the boys answer.

"Well, watch out for the riptide on the south end. It'll carry you right out into the Atlantic, and your poor mothers will never get to see their babies again!" the old guy continues.

"Yeah, thanks," Jack answers.

Henry loads the beer and groceries into the two metal coolers in the trunk.

Chapter 4

The Drive

"We'll put beer in one and groceries in the other. That'll keep it all fresh," Henry says.

The boys jump into the car, drive across the Wilmington Island River, and continue on what now becomes Tybee Road as they cross the bridge. Shrimp boats are lined up against the docks near Thunderbolt, and the seagulls are flying all around some of the boats, which have just come in from the Atlantic, and there is plenty to eat. Pelicans, by the dozens, fly and sit on pilings near the bridge.

Henry says, "The pelican's beak can hold more than its belly can!"

"Yeah, not Billy, though. His belly can hold more than anything can!" Lafayette quips.

"And your mouth can run longer than my sister's can!" Billy says back.

Lafayette grabs Billy by the neck and rubs his head with his knuckles as the DeSoto motors down the narrow two-lane Tybee Road. The road twists and turns until it reaches the Bull River Bridge, where a couple at a small eatery sells boiled crabs surrounded by a group of majestic low country oaks. The DeSoto slows, and the boys observe people lined up at the popular business to eat a dozen or more of the freshly cooked, orange-colored crustaceans and drink large glasses of sweet tea.

Henry recalls, as a boy, his mother telling him that the crabs do not feel a thing as they are dropped into the boiling water because they die instantly. His mother would boil water in a large metal pot on her gas-operated kitchen stove and allow Karl and him to drop the angry snapping crabs into the boiling water. He and Karl watched the crabs instantly succumb to the shock of the hot water. Occasionally, a feisty one would get away before being forced into the pot, and there would be bedlam on the kitchen floor until it was caught. And if it pinched you with one of its claws, you didn't forget!

He always thought it was a lot of work cleaning cooked crabs for the coveted white crab meat. But his mother patiently and efficiently picked the crab meat for him, his brother, and his dad. His mother was the best crab meat picker he knew; the meat always tasted better when she picked it. At home, a beer or two was always enjoyed with the crabs. He remembers his father saying, "It doesn't get any better than this, boys!" as he ate the crabs and drank his beer at the kitchen table covered with old Savannah newspapers. And so, it doesn't, Henry thought, especially after he had returned home from the service.

The Bull River Bridge is a favorite fishing spot, and fishermen are lined up near and along the bridge, as the boys cross the Bull River and resume their trip down the palm-lined highway. It was pretty much a straight shot to Tybee now that they had reached the bend in the road that led to the Lazaretto Creek Bridge. The roadbed was built through the miles of marshland that could be seen to the south. On the north side of the highway was the old railroad bed. The north channel leads ships to the safety of the port. Between the channels was Cockspur Island. The total trip by car from the mainland was about fourteen miles, giving Tybee Island a healthy separation from the City of Savannah, and the traveler a scenic drive. Beyond Tybee was the Atlantic Ocean and then Ireland, which Billy said he would like to sail to from Tybee.

"One day, I'll disappear, and you will know I'm at sea somewhere between Tybee and the Emerald Isle, fellows," Billy would sometimes say.

Billy's pals worried he might just do it, and in his worst moments, Henry thought he might join him. For now, anyway, the Savannah boys were all landlubbers.

"Don't hit any of the diamondback terrapins crossing the highway, Henry," Billy says.

"They cross US 80 in late spring and early summer," Lafayette responds.

"No, that's when they lay their eggs...the baby terrapins cross several months later. They're on their own right away and are trying to get to the marsh for their first meal." Billy observes. "They're crossing now," Billy adds.

"Henry just ran over one. Didn't you hear the crunch? That wasn't your run-of-the-mill turtle. That was a diamondback terrapin!"

"How do you know all this, Billy? You making stuff up again?" Laf asks.

"No, the man at Barbee's Pavilion at Isle of Hope told me. His family has a diamondback terrapin farm there," Billy responds. "He releases the females with eggs back into the marsh and then goes back to selling butter pecan ice cream to his customers."

Billy adds, "Terrapins, ice cream, and beer, that's what he does as he likes to say... and not necessarily in that order at the

Pavilion. He also told me the diamondbacks are the only terrapins that swim in saltwater."

"Yeah, I know that place. I didn't know what kind of turtles they were. You learn something new every day, but let me ask you, Billy. How did you know Henry ran over a diamondback terrapin and not a regular turtle? Do they make a special noise, too?" Laf asks.

"Just a good guess," Billy responds.

"No, definitely just an old box turtle, Laf," Henry adds as he drives. "Either I had to go into oncoming traffic, head into the marsh, or run over the turtle. Take your pick."

"Could have braked, Henry," Billy says.

"Don't trust the brakes on the old DeSoto for that kind of stop," Henry answers.

"Well, it's bad luck to run over a diamondback terrapin, Henry. It's like killing a cricket inside the house or a ladybug anywhere," Billy adds. "Guess it's all right to run over a box turtle or something by mistake but not a diamondback terrapin," Billy says again. "Maybe we should call ourselves the Terrapins," Billy suggests.

"How 'bout the Box Turtles?" Henry adds jokingly.

"More like the Loggerheads," Laf adds.

"Let's not go there, fellas," Jack says. "We are the Coastal Builders?"

Chapter 5

The Boys of Summer

The four boys in the DeSoto are to meet up with their buddy, Phil Keane, "at the beach." He would deliver pilings, lumber, nails, and such from Savannah for the one-room beach house. He arranged to drop off the order that morning, and they'd all unload the truck and begin the project borne out of a conversation at Jerry George's Soda Fount across from the boys' old high school on Bull Street the five had attended.

The four were back from the service after the last year of the war. Phil had been given an exemption but had served in the local Coast Guard Auxiliary, or CGA, as he sometimes called it, patrolling the Savannah waters for enemy saboteurs. He had even taken a watch in the WWII tower on the north end erected at the mouth of the Savannah River to look for German submarines trying to sneak into the Savannah River channel. By then, however, Germany had surrendered, but the Auxiliary kept up the war effort on the home front until the Bomb was dropped, and Japan also surrendered.

Phil likes to say he joined the "Coastal Defense Force." At sixteen, he patrolled the waterways in his little skiff while we

19

were still at war with Germany. German saboteurs could have been dropped off by German U-boats just like they were at Jacksonville Beach. The FBI busted them before they could blow up factories and planes and stuff. Phil even said an FBI agent from Savannah, Agent Lewis, had instructed their unit on how to handle a possible German saboteur if they happened upon one.

"The Germans were specially trained, Lewis told us, and the spies could blend in easily. They would even know who won the last World Series. He taught us some secrets to spotting them," Phil had explained.

Phil is just a decent guy, a gifted artist, spiritual, and always looking for a way to serve. Probably next to Billy, the best of us, Henry surmises. *They are both loyal guys with real character and an appreciation for what is really important.*

Billy asks, "Well, who won the Series last year?"

"Damn, Billy, you would be shot as a spy!" Lafayette exclaims.

"Well, Lafayette, who won it?" Billy exhorts.

"Er, huh...let me think a minute," Lafayette says.

"The Yankees," Jack answers.

"Yeah, the Yankees, you moron," Lafayette says to Billy.

The boys all laugh.

"I saw the Babe play an exhibition game with the Yanks at Grayson Stadium," Billy comments. "I was thinking about meeting the Babe when we passed the stadium a little while ago. I even got him to autograph one of those little bats they sometimes give away at the gate. He had a hard time signing the wood, so he sort of carved his signature into the bat. A genuine Babe Ruth carved signature. It will be worth hundreds one day!"

"Damn, Billy, the Great Savannah Races, the Babe...I guess

you talked to FDR when he came to Savannah before the War," Lafayette remarks.

"I said my Pop was at the Great Savannah Races, not me," Billy argues. "But I sold his Secret Service agents sodas when they stopped off at the Gingerbread House on Bull Street, and the president got out to admire the woodwork."

"I think they gave him one of the Coca-Colas I sold them," Billy adds. "That's when I had that bike with the basket on the front and..." Billy starts to explain.

"Yeah, we all remember that bike, Billy," Lafayette says.

"And how were things that day on the Missouri when the Japs surrendered to General MacArthur and the president? Did you wave and sell them sodas, too?" Lafayette asks sarcastically.

"No, wasn't there, Laf. Wasn't there at all," Billy replies.

The DeSoto continues east on the palm-lined highway.

"Each palm is planted for a soldier who was killed in WWI," one says.

"All from Georgia," another adds.

"All buried under a palm tree," one jokingly says.

"No, most buried in Europe," another remarks.

"Yeah, died fighting the Hun, and then we had to fight him again," another observes.

"They don't quit," Lafayette says.

"Like the Japs on Iwo Jima. They were dug in deep, and we couldn't get them out.

Nothing could get them out. Some are still on the islands and haven't surrendered.

To them, the war is still going on." Billy remarks.

"Fascists!" Lafayette yells.

"Now, the commies," Lafayette adds. "That's why I'm staying in the Reserves. Just in case the Huns rise up again and the Japs, too!"

"No, not going to happen for a long time, fellas," Henry observes. "They are beat," he says.

"And we're going to fish and drink beer and build a house where you can throw the fishing line into the tidal creek from the bed!" he exclaims.

You know the Kennys are related to the Waving Lady who waved to ships all those years with a handkerchief during the day and a lantern at night," Billy Burns observes as they pass Cockspur Island.

"Her pop was the lighthouse keeper on Elba Island just up the river some," Billy adds.

"Yeah, she's world famous now, but she died a few years back," Lafayette adds. "Billy could take her place if he moved near the north channel."

"Oh, I am the Waving Boy. Welcome to the Port of Savannah!" Billy says as he pulls out a plaid handkerchief from his work jeans and waves it out the rolled-down window of the DeSoto. The wind catches the piece of cloth, and it sails out onto Highway 80, which ends the career of the Waving Boy!

"Just as well, the ships would have all turned around and headed back out to sea anyway, Billy," Laf remarks.

The car passes old Fort Pulaski and Lafayette remarks, "The Confederates should have dug in like the Japs, and when those Yankees thought they had them whipped and entered the fort, they could have come out from the rubble and won the day!"

"No, Lafayette, the fort was about to explode. The rifled cannon was breaching the ammo supply. Nothing they could have done. The Montgomery Guards, an all-Irish regiment from Savannah, would have been annihilated, and you, Keane, Butler, and probably Billy wouldn't be here!" Henry says.

Henry thought of the stories he had heard in American History class at BC about the Confederate soldiers who would often retreat walking backward lest they get shot in the back and be mistaken as cowards running from the invading Yanks. Billy Burns called it "advance to the rear." He felt sad for those boys and guessed they must have had a lot of courage and balance to retreat, walking or running backward. Henry thought it must have been in their nature, just like the little fiddler crabs. Lafayette and Billy were such men. He and Jack? Well, he guessed he and his buddy were not cowards, but they would do what was expedient, and that would be to, if necessary, retreat expeditiously!

Sometimes, officers or the higher-ups behind desks really get it wrong. Even soldiers must be willing to think outside the box and retreat accordingly, advancing to the rear.

They pass is old golf course between the Post Theater and Officer's Row at Fort Screven.

"Bet it was like hitting out of a big sand trap since it was built on the dunes..." Jack says.

"I'd play well there, Jack, since I'm used to the city-run Muni and Union Bag's Mary Calder," Henry remarks.

"When you pass the bar exam, Henry, you can join the Savannah Golf Club," Jack adds.

"Yeah, when I graduate Armstrong and get accepted to law school, pass the bar, and make a little money. There are a lot of 'ifs,' Jack."

The lagoons remind Henry that pirates occasionally visited Tybee and would moor their stolen galleons and frigates off the beach and row to shore in small launches to hide their booty. Some hidden place up one of the little waterways or near a lagoon would have been where X marked the spot. Henry guessed it wouldn't be the beach. That would be too obvious. It had to be a lagoon. He and Billy, who liked to dig for old bottles, might one day find out.

"You know, Hussey's great grandfather, Lieutenant

Hussey, saved the colors on the parapet during the bombard-
ment," Lafayette states.

"What about you, Henry? Would you still be here had the
cannon fire breached the ammo supply?" Lafayette asks.

"My people are from Charleston, founded in 1670, over
sixty years before Savannah was founded as a buffer for
Charleston!"

"Sandlapper!" Lafayette responds.

"Sand crabs!" Henry says back.

"And damn sand gnats everywhere!" Butler adds.

The boys all laugh.

The black sedan takes the final bend to the Lazaretto Creek
Bridge—the bridge to Tybee. "Phil Keane calls this the 'final
bend' and 'the Bridge to Everywhere or the Bridge to
Nowhere," Henry says.

"He's such a poet and artist," Laf says sarcastically.

"Actually, he is," Henry says. "I've seen some of his stuff.
It's pretty good. He writes, draws and paints well," Henry
continues.

"Just doesn't always deliver lumber on time," Laf says.

"He will, Laf. Phil always comes through," Jack responds.

After crossing the bridge at Lazaretto Creek and arriving
on Tybee Island, the boys pass a little marina where shrimp
boats are moored and men are unloading crates filled with
Atlantic blue crabs onto pickup trucks headed into Savannah. All along the highway, people are selling crabs and
peaches in bushel baskets near the bridges. Their old pickups
with wooden guardrails in the bed become "rolling
stores." Men from up the country wear their blue jean over-
alls. Their wives wear white cotton linen dresses and oversized
straw hats, protecting their faces and body from the sun, which
is tamed by a gentle breeze of fresh salt air. One elderly lady
with an open umbrella sits in a chair watching her grandchil-

dren, not fishing. Cane pole fishers on the banks of the tidal creeks gather with their families. The kids anxiously watch for Mom, Dad, Grandma, and Grandpa to "reel in" a brim or spot from the brackish salt water. They are people etching out an honest living and catching dinner for their families.

"It's getting late in the season, but people still have to eat," Jack observes.

"Just like the Coastal Indians a thousand years ago," Lafayette remarks.

"That's why you find arrowheads and Indian pottery all over the place. Look where the cedar trees are. That's where they'd land their dugout canoes, have crab boils, and eat shell-fish," Lafayette observes.

Tourism is growing. The road really opened things up. The ferries and even the railroad are things of the past. The automobile brings thousands to the quiet little island packed with folks from Savannah, Augusta, up the country, the airmen from the SAC base near Savannah, young vets, students, and families. The Tybee business owners are ready, as they have had about six months to prepare during the off-season. They will work hard, make money, and hunker down until the season starts up again. Year after year, hordes of people leave the deserted island. Homes and cottages are sometimes boarded up for the winter. The bars, the local market, and little churches are usually the only places that seem to have any activity in the off-season. "Salt life," some are beginning to call it.

The old DeSoto carrying the Savannah group slows and turns onto the sandy dirt road leading to the "Lot" as it drives by several crab stands and juke joints. The dust from the road rises and covers the black sedan. The boys roll up the windows quickly, especially since a lone Model-A car speeds down the same road in the opposite direction.

"That's about as much traffic as we will see on this road,"

remarks Henry. "It's off the beaten path; in fact, it is a beaten path."

Henry eases the DeSoto down the narrow road with thick foliage on both sides. The Model-A passes, and the car windows are quickly rolled down again. The marsh can be seen through the subtropical vegetation. Then, there is a clearing where there is nothing but marsh and a little island or hammock in the distance.

Henry and Phil had found the Lot some weeks ago. They purchased it recently and closed the deal with Henry, Phil, Jack, Billy, and Lafayette, signing off on it and acquiring a share. They had scavenged about to gather the needed equipment and were anxious to have everything in one place so they could simply go to work on the project. They were waiting for Phil to make the big delivery of lumber and other things needed, like nails, cement mix, roofing, etc.

"You can't see the deep-water creek from the road, but it's there," Henry comments.

The Lot on the marsh and the little tidal creek, a tributary of Tybee Creek, is the domain of the Boys of the Summer of 1947.

Chapter 6

Juke Joints

A few marsh birds fly about, and the little hammock just sits there quietly, waiting for its new owners to hike through the marsh and land on its soil. The putrid smell of the salt marsh at low tide reveals the richness of its black mud as it absorbs decaying marsh grass, other vegetation, and marsh crustaceans and fish. Muscles and oysters create bubbling and gurgling sounds as the tide empties into the creeks and larger tributaries, eventually withdrawing into rivers and the Atlantic Ocean. The saltwater advances again with the incoming tide and fills to the top of the marsh grass.

Old timers blame "marsh gases" on mental illness, but more than likely, it is the high humidity of the southeast in the summer. It may very well contribute to forms of depression.

Henry has a friend whose father was placed in the State Mental Hospital in Milledgeville, where some volunteers unofficially referred patients from the Sea City as having been diagnosed with the "Savannah Syndrome." Henry figured it was marsh gases or the tendency for Savannahians from the sleepy southern port city to imbibe too much.

His friend's dad discovered he was well again once he returned to Savannah. "Don't worry about the marsh gases, but lay off the booze," he was told by his doctor.

The marsh continues to birth new sea life, like the ever-popular blue crab and shrimp that skim along the tops of its tidal creeks and feed the American herring, redfish, "The Lord of the Marsh," and other fish. The boys again note the quiet.

"Guess it's been like this since the beginning of time," Lafayette observes.

"A long time, but not since the beginning," Henry answers.

"All this was once covered by the ocean, and then the waters receded, and plants began to grow, and waterways were created by the currents, and here it is, since almost the beginning of time, Henry concludes.

The boys walk through the marsh as the tide is out. Later, they will wade back to the "mainland," as one jokingly calls it, as the tide comes in. For now, however, the builders begin to discuss where exactly the house will be placed, in which direction, where the pilings will be dug, and how many. Jack Butler unfolds the blueprints and surveys the little island.

Lafayette Adams, Henry McGee, and Billy Burns gather around him and look as he offers suggestions. They await Phil, the lumberman. The Boys of Summer have arrived and begin to make their moves.

"I guess we could have ordered a small house from the Sears catalog," Billy suggests.

"It's not the same, Billy," Lafayette answers. "This will be a custom-built house!"

"There it is! The lumber truck and Keane," Henry exclaims as Keane pulls up, blowing the horn.

"Scouting for Japanese mini-subs that haven't surrendered," Jack says jokingly.

"And Zeroes and Stuka bombers," Lafayette adds.

"Oh, lay off of him," Henry says.

"Yeah, it's not his fault he got rejected three times by all branches of the service. He wanted to fight. That's what's important," Lafayette says. "Had to do with his health. A lot of little things added up."

"You're right, fellows," Jack responds.

"His daddy got our plans approved with the Corps to build on that little hammock on our lot. Henry got the permit," Jack says.

"We're legal and ready to go, Coastal Builders!" Jack adds.

"Phil, the lumberman and artist!" The guys greet him, recognizing his immense artistic talents, which he recently used to win a contest to design a symbol that the city could use to encourage tourism.

"Should have copyrighted it, Phil," Henry had warned him.

Phil was an artist and lumberman, not an attorney, though. He didn't think people would just start using it without asking him first.

"Copyright," McGee had told him.

"C'est la vie," Phil had said.

The boys stand on the dirt road, looking out at the site of their new summer home. They are lords of all they survey.

"There it is. The place we will spend the rest of our summer and beyond," they all say.

"Let's go to work," they say again.

The boys unload some of the supplies from the overfull trunk of the DeSoto, partially opened and tied with a rope. The supplies include shovels, hand-held weeding sickles, much-needed hammers, a level, carpenter aprons, and a nail puller. The precious cargo of cold beer and sandwiches had also been removed.

The boys also begin to unload the pilings and lumber from the truck, and it isn't long before they open a few bottled beers. The Tybee weather is hot and humid. They were used to hard work, though, and were lean and tough because of it. While Adams, Burns, and Keane unload, Jack and Henry review the plans and try to organize the group. They join in as soon as they are done. "Don't watch people work—always join in if you can." That's their motto. They are lifting and giving orders as both tend to be leaders. They seem, at times, to almost be competing; at least, that was what Henry always thought. Neither made it overseas during the war. After graduating high school, Jack and Henry enlisted in the US Navy. They figured at least they'd get a clean bunk until the long-rumored invasion took place.

Billy and Laf are a little older. They were pulled from high school and saw some action in northern Africa and the Pacific. Neither of them told many war stories, so Jack and Henry guessed they had seen some action and just wanted to forget about it and move on with their lives. Laf simply said he marched through North Africa and Italy at nineteen and was glad he was home in Savannah.

Billy would occasionally mention the flamethrower story, and Jack and Henry felt he was haunted by the thought that there could have been women and children in the tunnels he torched. Henry had recommended he talk to one of the priests at Sacred Heart, so he did, and the priest told him to pray for their souls at Mass. Billy figures it must have been a sin of some kind or another since he was given a penance, so he prays for them but wonders who they are and when he must quit praying.

However, the chaplain told him, "You made the best decision you could at the time, and you did your duty." That made him feel a little better but didn't erase things. He figured he'd try to lead a good life from there on out. Lafayette thought the same but also felt he was born "to protect," so if he had the opportunity to serve again, he would. Jack and Henry told stories of the service and enjoyed it. All in all, they were young men who were maturing rapidly into full adulthood, assuming responsibility, and looking forward to pursuing their education and careers and having families of their own. For now, however, they were together for the rest of the summer.

They worked all day, took a short break for lunch, and now it was time for dinner or "knocking off time." They are beat and had been bitten by lots of mosquitos, sand gnats, and marsh flies, so they are ready to get some crabs or burgers and a few more beers.

They could walk to one of the juke joints on US 80. No one would bother their car since the old man in the little marsh shack kept coming out to check the boys' progress. He was an old salt and liked that he might have neighbors who seemed like good boys and all vets of one kind or another, patriotic Americans. He says he'd keep an eye on the lumber and the beer as he laughed. The boys think, *NO beer left, Grandpa.*

"Let's go get dinner," one says.

"And beer," Billy and Lafayette say together.

"And girls," Lafayette adds.

They all laugh because they and their clothes are a sight.

"They're laid back at Tybee. People are more casual and often wear work clothes, from fishing in the marshes and creeks, fixing up old houses, swimming at the beach, crabbing on the docks, and running in squalls. They might wear their Sunday best for Church services, but not the rest," Lafayette comments.

"And Lafayette's a poet and doesn't know it," Henry quips.

"Girls are the same everywhere; they want you smelling nice, Adams, and right now we don't smell too nice," Butler says.

"Maybe Grandpa will let us shower at his place. I saw one outside," Billy remarks.

"That's for later, Billy; we got to get to know him better and offer him a few beers," Henry says.

The boys walk to Jake's, a two-story cinder block building near the sandy road and US 80. Lots of folks are there, drinking and eating crabs, burgers, and hot dogs from an open-pit barbecue that operates out front near the covered eating area. The jukebox plays the Harmonicats' new hit, "Peg O' My Heart," and the Irish American boys love it.

"We're home, fellas!" Butler exclaims.

Families are gathered at wooden picnic tables. Workers, dirtier than them, are enjoying a few Pabst beers. People are laughing and talking and happy.

"Life doesn't get any better than this," Henry observes.

"Yeah, this is America, boys!" Lafayette adds.

"Three dozen blue crabs and five Pabsts," the boys call out to the lady working the tables.

"Why five?" one of the boys asks, "Keane went home."

"Oh, hadn't noticed," Lafayette responds.

"All right, in honor of Phil Keane, lumberman. He always comes," Henry says.

"Yeah, and to the Coast Guard Auxiliary," the boys laugh.

"Yeah, but Phil had a Section 8 he's real sensitive about. They just wouldn't take him, melancholic or something," Butler comments.

"Jack's right. Phil tried everything to get in, fellas; let's lay off him for good. He served in the best way he could," Henry adds.

The Pabsts arrive.

"To Phil Keane!" they all raise their longneck bottles.

"Jake is making some money now," Jack observes.

"He'll need it for the winter," Henry responds.

The boys begin to sing the lyrics of "Peg O My Heart" to the cheers of the crowd. Everyone is happy and laughing.

"A regular Irish pub off the coast of Savannah!" Butler observes.

The boys walk "home" late to the Lot, singing another rendition of "Peg O' My Heart." Suddenly, Jack and Henry break out in an old song from their Navy days.

"I joined the Navy to see the world! And what did I see? I saw the sea! I saw the Atlantic... I saw the Pacific, but the Atlantic wasn't romantic, and the Pacific wasn't what it was cut out to be!"

Henry and Jack sleep in the car underneath Army surplus mosquito nets, the other two in a lean-to on the hammock with a fire to keep the bugs away. Phil had to get back early to the lumberyard and would try to thumb a ride to the Lot tomorrow. The others will work through the weekend and return to Savannah on Sunday in the DeSoto.

The moon is full, and the tide is unusually high. The ocean waters reach the tops of the marsh grass, and the little hammock is surrounded by water and truly appears as an island.

The boys camped on the hammock are like marooned seamen left stranded with little resources to survive until a passing ship appears on the horizon or a low-flying rescue plane flies over them to save the day. The light of the moon shines bright on the waters and the tops of the marsh grass. It is hard to see where the creek runs and the marsh begins. All the waters come together. The grass and the water sparkle like thousands of clear little votive candles lit for a procession. The water glistens, giving it a white-gold coloring that reflects heavenward.

The boys rest peacefully until Billy, true to form, breaks the grand silence and lets out a howl, looking to the full harvest moon, "Ah-oooh!"

Then, they all sleep soundly, exhausted by manual labor and sedated by the hops.

The air is steamy; there is no breeze. Strange sounds come from the marsh and creek. Long streamlined birds soar silently through the air like gliders and land in the marsh grass, making little noises that sound much different than the chirping birds in Savannah.

Fish could be heard splashing in the water, a hoot owl in the distance, other unidentifiable noises occurring as the tide moves in and out, and the little waves splashing against the marsh mud. The Boys of Summer are oblivious to it all as they are exhausted. They sleep soundly, except for an occasional slapping of a mosquito or gnat. The fire and surplus mosquito nets help the boys deal with the millions of flying insects that fill the darkness and rule the wetlands.

The Boys of Summer are even too tired for dreams, but they know they are living one of them.

Henry and Jack are awakened by Billy yelling, "Help, help, we're marooned on a deserted island. Help, we are marooned!"

As the two men get out of the DeSoto, they see that the tide has come in, and the hammock is surrounded by high water. It is getting ready to ebb, but Billy wants to get a sandwich out of the cooler. He and Lafayette are thirsty and hungry.

"You're a marine, Billy. TAKE the beach!" yells Jack.

"A little water never hurt anyone," Henry hollers out.

Lafayette simply lies there and asks for water and aspirin from the car. Billy jumps into the water and wades to shore. He gets the needed supplies and wades back.

"The Marines have landed. The Army Air Corps is rescued again!" Billy cries.

"Yes, I'm wounded, Marine, 'shell-shocked' from the constant barrage of fire. A concussion, too," Lafayette moans.

"Yeah, from the SS Pabst," Henry says.

"I need a priest," Lafayette calls out.

"The chaplain is tending to the dying. Adams, make your confession to the Marine.

He can tell the chaplain," says Jack.

"Up and at-um, fellows. Times, a-wastin'. Hit the deck!" Henry yells as he plays revelry with an invisible bugle.

The troops rally, boil some water for coffee on the fire, eat the last of the sandwiches, and drink the water from the cooler.

Lafayette has a beer and feels better.

"Let's get this done!" he hollers in a commanding voice, and all the boys go to work.

The holes for the pilings are dug deep, and after some prep work, the large round timbers are placed into the sandy dirt of the hammock. The cement is hand-mixed on a piece of plywood with a flat shovel. Sand and cement mixed with water are added to make a sludge-like concrete. It is shoveled into the holes around the pilings, along with some old hangers, to hold the cement together and add stability. It is hard work in the mid-day Georgia sun, and the accumulated heat is "oppressive" at the end of the day. The light breezes from the marshes and waterways are welcome visitors from nature.

The young vets are strong and have stayed in reasonably good shape. They still get together to play basketball in front of Henry McGee's house, as they have done for years. Occasionally, they will play a round of golf at "Muni," the public course in Savannah, or Mary Calder Golf Course, the nine-hole course out near Union Bag, where some of their fathers work. Games such as this help them continue to hone their athletic skills and reflexes, along with the regular games of half-rubber in the warmer months and touch football in the winter.

And the basketball games at Lincoln and Maupas are year-round.

Manual labor is done around the house and neighborhood. They have part-time physical jobs and a day on the water, casting for shrimp. All these things keep the Boys of Summer lean and strong. For most of them, going to college and studying constantly exercises their brain muscles, they hope.

After the cement dries, the 2x8s are nailed into the pilings, and the flooring planks go on "one at a time," as Laf orders. The 2x4s for the frame will be nailed to the flooring.

The framing will be tricky, but several of the boys have done it before. It will be raised and secured properly. Afterward, the rafters for the roof will be individually placed. The boys will continue to work as a team, as was their training in high school military classes, sports teams, clubs, and organizations. The service helped perfect their ability and the necessity to work with others. Lafayette is a real carpenter; the rest learn fast and provide more brawn. A level is constantly used to ensure the house remains square. There is little room for horseplay, especially since the Boys of Summer will soon be the Boys of Fall!

"Let's get this flooring done, the framing up, and the rafters on, and cover this thing," one of the boys suggests.

"The roof can be put on after the siding," another says.

"Listen, we need a covering for the rain. I'm already tired of getting soaked by these squalls coming off the ocean," another says.

So the boys will go with covering the rafters with plywood first, then the black roofing paper, and finally, the light gray colored shingles. "The fun part," Billy calls it. He explains how to drive the little roofing nails into the roofing paper and then shingles. "I hear experienced roofers can spit these little nails out of their mouths and hit them once with a hammer, and that's it."

"Please, Billy, don't try it," Jack pleads. "Or you, Henry," he adds.

"Yeah, we'd swallow one," Henry says.

"Yeah, and then we'd waste a nail, Henry," Laf remarks.

"Or an esophagus, if you know what that is, Laf," Henry responds.

"Yeah, that's another name for your brain, Henry," Laf answers.

All laugh as Henry sings a rendition of the scarecrow's song in *The Wizard of Oz*, "If I only had a brain."

He concludes by saying to Laf, "Yes, you are the brains now, Lafayette Adams. The rest of us can't even drive a nail straight!" Laf delights in his newfound status and that his friends publicly acknowledge his skills.

After the cement dries, the work proceeds fast. The boys will soon enjoy a dry night in a few days or so, except when the squalls come in and it rains sideways. Yes, the roof will be put on before the siding. They all agreed to the plan, although Jack seems slightly leery. Henry would realize one day soon that Jack's instincts were right. Jack didn't press the issue, so he got on board with the change. They will enjoy a cover on their partially built house—at least for a while.

"It will sure be nice sleeping on the new floor of this house with a room," Billy comments one night as the boys all fall asleep around the construction site with a fire to keep the bugs away and add a little light.

"Yeah, and at least we know it has room for us all," Henry says.

"What about the wife and kids?" Jack asks.

Henry replies, "Let's not even go there."

"Amen," Phil adds.

"We need to go over everything. What we'd say in the Navy, Henry?" Jack asks.

"Batten down the hatches," the two Navy vets say simultaneously and laugh.

"Really, though, it's detail work and maybe tedious, but it has to be done," Jack reiterates.

"My work will hold, Butler," Lafayette says, half awake.

"We will sleep on the flooring soon and put up a tarp if it rains and the mosquito nets. We can keep the fire on the hammock burning..." Henry says.

"And sing camp songs," Billy adds.

"And NOT sing camp songs," Henry and Jack say together.

Both had worked in the Catholic Camp at Isle of Hope near Savannah in high school.

"Cheer, cheer for Villa Marie. We are the campers happy and free." The tune matched the Notre Dame fight song.

Jack sang the Georgia Tech fight song as he hoped to one day be an engineer. "I'm a rambling wreck from Georgia Tech, a helluva an engineer."

The "helluva" part got Jack in trouble when one of the campers told the nuns and priest director that Jack was cursing. Jack remembers explaining to the good sister, "Sister, it's just a cheer song," not wanting to call it a "fight song." But here, it was fine. Their own home away from home—a beach house.

When they ran into one of the Benedictine priests and told the good monk about their plans, he called it "a retreat house."

"Yeah, a retreat house for young men returning from the war, Father," Jack said.

"My work will hold," Laf says again as he falls into a restful slumber. The others soon start snoring.

The house on the hammock, their beach house retreat, will soon stand high and proud, rising out of the marshes of Tybee Island.

Chapter 7

Innocent Pedestrians

Day after day, the boys work long and hard as the days turn into weeks. The Gang of Four: Henry, Jack, Billy, and Laf decide it's about time for a real day and night off so they head to The Strand before the season closes. "It should still be hoppin' on the weekend," they say.

Tybee was essentially divided into three general areas: the Strand, the Back River, and Fort Screven. The Strand is the business district along the beach, where there are hotels, motels, restaurants, bars, and stores that sell beach supplies and hardware. The Back River was a quiet neighborhood for families and people wanting to escape the crowded beach and noise, although it had been much louder since they had arrived. Fort Screven had been a part of the Coastal Defense System at the turn of the century but was obsolete now, especially with radar, aircraft carriers, and jets.

Grandpa joins the boys again around the DeSoto. They thank him for looking after things and ask him to join them for a beer around the construction site later.

"Sorry, fellas. The tide will be coming in again. You better plan on getting wet. Thanks, though," the old man responds.

Grandpa was an old salt and would be a good neighbor for the few years he had left. He walks with a cane, can't see or hear well, and coughs a lot as he sometimes puffs on a corncob pipe. When he smokes it, he always has to light it with his Zippo, which burns more of the cob than the tobacco.

"Careful of them boys from up the country, fellows. They like to fight more than you," he warns.

"If they start something, walk away. Ain't no one down here knows you, and there ain't no shame in that," the old salt counsels. "But if you have to, take 'em out quick 'cause they won't stop until they drop. Prideful young men, they are," he adds.

"Thanks, Grand, er, I mean..." Lafayette starts to say.

"'Grandpa' is okay, but the name is Cobb, Mr. Cobb," he laughs as he holds up his burnt cob pipe.

The boys head up to US 80 and easily hitch a ride to Butler Avenue. They get out just around the dogleg, where the ocean can be seen. Sometimes, waves come up splashing against the big granite boulders during a storm at high tide. Crowds of people now appear. They are near the Mediterranean-style hotel, The Desoto, a Tybee landmark.

"DeSoto must have been important," Billy observes. "He has a car, a hotel in Savannah, and one at Tybee named after him."

"The Spanish were the first Europeans here, Billy. A long time before the English," Lafayette states. "This was all part of Florida once."

"The Yuchi Indians were first, though," Henry adds.

"Yeah, reckon they were," Lafayette replies.

The boys have chosen the right place for an evening off as a festive atmosphere prevails. There are lots of families. It is not dusk yet, but lights begin to go on and Butler Avenue seems even more alive. The postwar boom is in full swing. "To Each His Own" by Freddie Martin and his orchestra is playing on a nearby jukebox, followed by Perry Como singing "Prisoner of Love" on another.

"I want to be a prisoner of love," Billy says as he walks along palm-lined Butler Avenue past the old DeSoto Hotel and Victorian-style beach houses.

Phil and Henry cross themselves as they reach St. Michael's Catholic Church, noting the Mass times are 8 a.m. and 11 a.m. Billy lifts his St. Christopher medal out from his shirt and kisses it.

"His prayers got me back home," Billy says, "and he'll see me the rest of the way."

Henry wears the medal, too. The one his mother gave him. It's sterling and attached to a strong silver chain around his neck. The medal is the Miraculous Medal of Our Lady of Lourdes in Lourdes, France. Henry thinks the prayers of the Blessed Mother are strong, and between her and Jesus, he is in good hands.

"We'll hear the 11:00 a.m. Mass," a couple of the boys say, almost in unison. Sunday Mass is just part of their lives, and they and their friends know that is where they will be each Sunday morning. Whether they go to Communion or not, it doesn't matter. They'll be there asking forgiveness and trying to do better in the coming week. They believe firmly that the Mass is the anchor of their week. In fact, there are old anchors here and there about Tybee used for decorating lawns and the front of businesses. Henry thinks it represents not only seafarers like him and Jack but also the virtue of hope like the nuns taught him.

"Without the Holy Sacrifice, we are adrift, Mother McGee says," Henry comments.

The American Catholic sailors and soldiers of all different backgrounds and parentages marched together to Mass while stationed in Italy. Lafayette Adams remembers hundreds of US soldiers hearing Mass in a local church, where mostly the women and old men went. The young Italian men were so impressed that they, too, began to show up the following weekend.

"I always thought I'd done something good when that happened," Lafayette says.

"You were a true 'soldier of Christ' like when you were confirmed," Jack says.

"Yeah, a real soldier and a soldier of Christ," Lafayette responds.

The boys walk past St. Michael's down to 12th Street when a deep baritone voice with a Geechee accent hollers out from an upstairs screened porch. "McGee, Burns, Butler, and Adams...up to no good!"

The boys look around frantically, and a deep male voice laughs heartily, calling out, "What, a guilty conscience?"

Lafayette, always ready for a fight to defend his honor or the honor of his family and friends, looks up to the porch of the two-story Tybee beach house and starts to laugh aloud, observing, "It's just 'Billy Edward Hayes' without anything to do except holler at innocent pedestrians!"

"Innocent?" Billy Edward Hayes asks, laughing. "Pedestrians? And where'd you learn that fifty-cent word, Adams? Parking cars at the courthouse? I think I'll call the Tybee police on you knuckleheads now; it will save everyone some time."

Billy Edward Hayes is a friend of Lafayette Adams' older brother and Karl McGee. He graduated from Commercial High across from BC on Bull Street and hung out at the BC armory. He is considered an "honorary alumni" of BC, and he now helps coach aspiring basketball players from the neighborhood. He is one of those guys who seems to know everyone and could turn up anywhere. He, too, was a vet and, like so many, is looking for a future in the sleepy little southern port city. But for now, he is pulling the Savannah group's chain. The boys know, however, that Billy Edward would be the first to their rescue. "He has character," Henry McGee's dad would say.

Chapter 8

Watch the Riptide and Skip the Jetties

The "innocent pedestrians" continue down the palm-lined Butler Avenue towards the Tybee Hotel. The boys pass the Fresh Air Home, which Lafayette likens to summer reform school like the Marist Brothers School in Savannah. "Send them to the Brothers," the Catholics would say of a boy who was "incorrigible."

"The Brothers will certainly straighten them out!" the old folks would reiterate.

"I don't think the delinquents go to the Fresh Air Home, but maybe The Marist Brothers' School," Henry quips.

Both institutions encourage youth. They give young people hope and faith. Charity would come later. The Marist Brothers call them "the three theological virtues."

Another old hotel and retreat called the Georgianne is just up ahead, and Lafayette remarks, "When I get married and have a little girl, I'm going to name her Georgianne Adams."

Jack Butler observes, "That's not a saint's name...Gotta have a saint's name."

"Neither is Lafayette," Henry observes.

"Lafayette was a lover of Lady Liberty, like me, so he's a saint," Laf responds.

"And Georgianne?" Jack asks.

Lafayette answers, "St. George slayed dragons, and Anne was Mary's mother. You don't get more saintly than that. Besides, my girl will be the first saint named Georgianne. Just got to keep her away from the Butlers."

Jack responds, "What you really mean, Laf, is that you gotta keep her away from guys like you!"

All the boys, including Lafayette, laugh.

They continue past the Tybee Hotel, where the big band sound can be heard coming out from the dance floor, down the covered walkway, into its beachside "courtyard," and all the way to Butler Avenue. A small part of the old railroad depot can still be seen in front of the grand hotel, which proudly flies the American flags from each of its twin pink stucco towers.

A traveling carnival is open near the hotel in an empty lot. It features a Ferris wheel spinning round and round, a colorful circling carousel ride, bumper cars, and other rides, especially for kids. The carnival sells confections like cotton candy, funnel cake with powdery sugar on top, candy apples, and lots more from booths scattered around the grounds.

"The games are all rigged," Laf notes.

"The ring toss is impossible, the basketball hoop is too small for the basketball, the sites on the rifle are way off… everything is rigged," Laf says again.

"They ain't getting my money," Laf adds.

The boys decide to skip the carnival, but people are having fun, laughing, and spending the extra money everyone seems to be making these days.

"You see, Laf, that's the fun and challenge of a carnival!" Jack says.

"Yeah, right," the savvy Laf replies.

"The carnies got to make money too, Laf; they're not in it for charity," Jack says again.

"Let's listen to the big band sound and have pretzels and beer instead," Billy interjects.

The carnival music fades as they continue south on Butler Avenue to 16th Street and the "real entertainment."

The boys continue south on Butler Avenue as they walk from the Tybee Hotel towards 15th and 16th Streets. The traffic is getting heavier, and Henry even notices a few Chrysler DeSoto cars just like his. *That's a good sign*, Henry thinks to himself. *Hernandez DeSoto was all over the Southeast and so is the automobile named after him.*

The crowds are increasing now. Mothers wearing beach robes and fathers in swim trunks return to their cars, carrying chairs and beach umbrellas with their children in tow. The youngsters will sleep well tonight, exhausted from running after seagulls and back and forth to the ocean, emptying buckets filled with seawater into hand-dug moats around little sandcastles.

A young boy carries a large black tire inner tube with patches on it that he was using to paddle out into the surf and ride the waves onto the beach until it became partially deflated. Other adults have already returned to their Tybee homes and hotel/motels, washing themselves of the sand and seawater of a day at the beach. They are now walking about in their night-out clothes. The ladies are in long white cotton print dresses, striped skirts, and white blouses, and the men are in light-colored dress shirts, pleated khakis, and grey flannel trousers. The older men wear ties and suspenders. A few even have their sports-coats or suit-coats on. Others carry them over their shoulders or fold them over their left arm, wiping their brow with handkerchiefs with their right hand.

Except for a few crying children leaving the beach late,

tired, and with too much sun, most people smile and laugh as they walk in and out of the bars and cafes on Butler Avenue between 15th and 16th Streets. Music from the jukeboxes at some bars and lounges can be heard, and a live big band sound flows through the air.

As Henry and his buddies approach 16th Street, they run into Jeff Woods or, as Jeff likes to remind folks, Jefferson Davis Woods or J.D. for short. Jeff is from an old Savannah family that is mostly Irish in heritage. The Woods always wanted acceptance in Savannah society and were likelier to name their children after dead Confederate generals than saints. They would claim distant relatives among the early founders of the country, southern war heroes, writers, and portraitists. The truth was that they were of peasant stock, just like almost everyone else.

As one local legend has it, Jeff's grandfather was allegedly a colonel in the Confederate army and had fought with General Lee and the Army of Northern Virginia at Gettysburg. "Survived Pickett's Charge, he did," the Woods all would say. The real story is that Jeff's great-grandfather was a private at Fort Pulaski, where General Lee had been temporarily assigned as a young officer long before Private Woods arrived on the scene. Private Woods deserted and was trying to return to Savannah when he was found wandering around Cockspur Island near Fort Pulaski hungry, muddy, and eaten up by mosquitoes. He claimed to be reconnoitering the island for the Yankees. He was sent north as a POW with the other soldiers when the fort fell and ended up as a chaplain assistant to Father Peter Whalen, the Irish-born chaplain at Fort Pulaski, who felt sorry for the young lad who seemed "a little touched."

Private Woods lived a long time once he returned home after the war. As a generation passed and memories seemed to fade, Private Woods claimed to be a colonel and a war hero. He would even show up at civic events in an old Confederate officer's uniform wielding a saber.

One day, during the annual Confederate Memorial Day Parade, he was giving a speech on a temporary outside stage when he began to wave the saber like he said he did during Pickett's Charge festivities. The swinging saber accidentally scratched the face of one of the women present, who fainted after the blood trickled down her cheek and dropped on her white blouse. As she lay on the stage bleeding, several other women fainted as well. It took a moment before it was discovered that the woman the colonel had cut was the mayor's wife. He was forced to surrender his saber to the city fathers, who committed him to a local sanatorium for "an assault on southern womanhood."

The mayor's wife told the story for the rest of her days and said the "Madman Private Woods" had cut her!

It was also said that when Mr. Woods was escorted to the sanitarium by men in white, "Colonel Woods" tried to holler out the rebel yell. Perhaps, the last rebel yell of a Confederate vet. "Woo, woo, woo," ending in a whimper. The War Between the States had finally ended for Private Woods, and he spent the rest of his days measuring the volume of birds, rabbits, squirrels, and whatever other critters wandered or flew onto the property of the mental institution.

The Woods forgot that Southerners have long memories, and the true story about the colonel was passed down, as well as the embellished one the Woods all presented, which no one believed. "They are decent enough people," Henry's father would say, "but a little touched." Henry guessed that was a nice way of saying, "They were nuts."

Of course, Jeff, who was always looking for respectability, starts explaining to Henry and the others that he's at Tybee on business. He tells them he is doing research for a novel he is writing about Tybee during the seizure of Fort Pulaski and wants to get a sense of the island and its people.

Henry tells him, "Jeff, it's better to do something like that during the off-season. Most of the people here now aren't from Tybee."

Jeff says, "Oh, I already know that, but seeing as the Yankee soldiers were from somewhere else and were sort of like visitors, I was hoping to channel some of that energy during the tourist season."

The other guys just drift away from Jeff. Henry asks, "Are you talking about the North Channel, where the ships come in and out of or what?"

"No. I gave you more credit than that. I'm talking about channeling energy from the past."

"Remember the physics lesson at BC where we learned that 'energy is neither created nor destroyed'? I'm talking about energy, McGee, energy!" Jeff the Touched yells out.

"Good luck with that, Jeff. I've got to catch up with the others. Don't, uh, I mean, join us for a beer at one of the bars on 16th Street if you'd like," Henry says.

"One of those places? I'd never go in one of those places. That's for the riffraff!" Jeff remarks and then turns and disappears into the crowd.

"Well, you might gain insight into the common folk if you had a beer with us, Jeff," Henry whispers as the future novelist walks away. Henry catches up with his friends who are on 16th Street.

"Hey, Henry, did Woods ever discover the volume of a rabbit?" Lafayette asks.

"What do you mean?" Henry answers.

"You ain't never heard that story? Let me tell you over a beer. Pick a bar, Billy," Lafayette calls out.

"Miller's Soda Shop on the corner of 16th and Butler," answers Billy.

"I meant a real bar, Billy. We aren't here to eat Sealtest ice cream, not tonight. We ought to send you back to Savannah on the Blue and White bus from Millers Soda Shop," Laf comments.

The boys go into a bar named Yunk's Place. They avoid the Riptide further down on 16th Street, heeding the warning of the old man at Duane's, "Watch the Riptide." They also skip "Jetty's" as Laf half-jokingly makes fun of the two bars' names. "One will yank you out to sea; the other will jettison you apart." Really, both are crowded, but a little superstition sets in on the Savannah group.

Billy observes, "The riptide yanks you out to sea, right?"

Henry answers, "That's right, Billy."

Billy observes again, "The jetties tear you apart, right?"

Henry answers cautiously, slowly, sensing Billy's building up to something, "Yes...they can..."

"And that's taking all this superstitious stuff too far. Even my Irish grandmother wouldn't go for that!" Jack adds.

"We're going into Yunk's, and that's final."

Yunk's is a typical walk-in off-the-street place with a long bar where several old salts, almost all resembling Grandpa, sit, drinking beer and whiskey.

"Some of Grandpa's chums," Henry says.

"And customers," Lafayette remarks.

There are a few tables off to the side, and next door, there is a small liquor store connected to the bar by a door. Smoke from cigarettes fills the air, and the opened door and ceiling fans allow some ventilation. It is dark. A jukebox plays the song "There's a White Cross on Okinawa" by some country singer.

"There's a white cross on Okinawa..." Billy gets agitated as he listens to the lyrics.

"Four Pabst!" Laf hollers out at the bartender.

"The volume of a rabbit?" Henry asks Lafayette.

"Oh yeah, well, Butler and I are at Woods' house one day, and Jeff has this rabbit cage in the back of the house, pulled the thing out of the cage, and is trying to measure it with a measuring tape. We ask Woods what the hell is he doing, and he says, 'I'm trying to determine the volume of a rabbit!'" Laf exclaims, and he and the others start laughing.

Jack Butler says, "True story, Henry."

"Not the end, not the end, fellas. Listen to me," Laf interjects.

His mother comes out looking for her measuring tape. We tell her what Jeff is trying to do, and she looks at him and says scoldingly, "Jeff, why can't you be like other boys?!"

The boys all laugh and shake their heads.

"The volume of a rabbit had something to do with geometry class," Laf adds.

"The boy's definitely not playing with a full deck."

"The smoke doesn't go all the way to the top of the chimney..." Jack agrees.

Billy listens intensely and finally asks, "Well, what is the volume of a rabbit?"

Henry shakes his head and simply thinks to himself, Poor Jeff; he is a nut.

Just as Lafayette finishes his story, a commotion is heard in front of Yunk's Place. Billy runs out immediately to investigate.

"Fight!" Billy comes back inside and hollers. Lafayette takes a final swallow of his beer and runs outside ahead of Billy.

"Blue Jackets and some boys from Cobbtown!" Billy yells again.

Lafayette is already in the middle of it as he knows the boys from High School who go there with his younger brother, who got expelled from BC for being "incorrigible."

He is taking the offensive and has the Cobbtown boys backed up. The High School Blue Jackets gain extra courage and move forward after being pressed against the wall. Billy, nicknamed the "Tank" on his high school football team, joins Lafayette. "These guys are ex-Marines!" the high schoolers yell, and the boys from up the country hesitate but don't back down.

They're just like Grandpa says they are: "prideful," Laf thinks, but he respects their tenacity. Lafayette knows he's got to take 'em out quick, just like Grandpa told him because their pride won't allow them to run.

Lafayette feels winded and hears Billy breathing hard, too. Too many smokes, he thinks.

A Benedictine kid by the name of Frank McKinney, or "Skinny" as some call him, recognizes the alumni and tries to help out. Skinny McKinney is a tall, gangly, red-headed high school junior. What Skinny lacks in brawn, he makes up for in courage.

Another High School kid, a big, strong boy by the name of Sonny, joins in the fray.   The adversaries are about evenly numbered now. The older boys are inspired and continue to fight back. They all hear sirens and see police lights and the crowd parting for the officers. Now, they all run.

The police grab several country boys and a High School boy named Sonny. The rest of the High School boys, assisted by the BC boys and the vets, disappear into the crowd and down the lane next to the Wilson Hotel on 16th Street. They escape.

Skinny slips out easily through the crowd.

Just as the BC and High School guys duck into the little lane next to the hotel, a large man in a white T-shirt and dark green work khakis suddenly appears. Henry recognizes the man as Howard Krapf. Mr. Krapf is Henry's neighbor. He has property on Izlar Avenue, one lane over from 16th Street, where Henry has stayed before with Mr. Krapf's family and his son, Richard, who is Henry's friend. Mr. Krapf is a local legend having been an outstanding lineman at Savannah High and having played college football for both the Citadel in Charleston and the University of Georgia in Athens. The Philadelphia Eagles had even offered him a contract; instead, Mr. Krapf elected to stay in the Savannah area, care for his ailing mother, and raise a family. He has even been nominated recently for the Jewish Athletic Hall of Fame.

Mr. Krapf grabs one of the High School boys by the scruff of the neck. He recognizes Henry and asks him, "What'd these boys do, Henry?" as the high school kid hangs dangling from one of Mr. Krapf's outstretched arms, running in place and swinging his arms in midair to no avail.

"A High School kid who got in a little scuffle, Mr. Krapf. It's nothing," Henry replies.

"Well, if it's nothing, I can let him go. If it was robbery, I'd give you a good thrashing, son, do you understand that?" Mr. Krapf adds as he shakes the young man, still dangling in midair.

"Yes, sir!" the high school kid hollers out in a high-pitched voice.

"Not a robbery?" Mr. Krapf asks. "No, sir," Henry answers.

Mr. Krapf then drops the brawler. The High School kid falls to the ground, gets up, and "heads for the territory," having dealt with tough country boys, the strong arm of the law, and now, Mr. Howard Krapf. To Henry, Mr. Krapf was "the kindest of men," but to ruffians, he was a force to be reckoned with.

"You be careful around here, Henry. Those boys from up the country like to come down here and pick fights," Mr. Krapf advises.

"I will, Mr. Krapf…and I'll look out for those knuckleheads

from the city, too," Henry adds as he looks around for Billy and Lafayette.

"You're right, Henry. Knuckleheads. All knuckleheads!" Mr. Krapf agrees.

The Tybee Island police lieutenant, assisted by several patrolmen, hollers out, "Unless you want thirty days on the chain gang and a $100 fine, behave yourselves!"

All get the message, and a calm quickly falls upon the crowd. People go back to acting civil and enjoying each other.

Henry still remembers the fight he got into a few years ago in Daffin Park, the place he had almost drowned as a young boy. Three boys accosted him and were going to give him a good thrashing for no good reason, so Henry reasoned a little with them.

"Fair enough if you think this park is yours, but to make it fair for me and you, let me take you one at a time."

The three agreed, and Henry started fighting one of the bigger of the three, telegraphing his punches, waiting to land a right jab to the nose, which he did. Blood came gushing out, and the boy ran, going into shock. The other two scattered, and Henry slipped away, too, worrying that he had either killed or knocked out an eye in the big guy.

Thankfully, he never saw them together in that park after that night. Don't want to kill anyone at this point in my life, he concluded.

Jack Butler was the same type of rational person. He got jumped by a gang in the park once and took a licking. Jack took care of that situation. He had memorized their faces and caught them one at a time. Took him months, but he did it. Never even mentioned the incident to his brothers. Took care of things by himself. He did tell Henry, though, and Henry thought he did the right thing.

Neither, though, would hesitate to rescue a family member or friend in trouble.

Henry figures he's had guys rescue him, like in the Navy at the end of the war. The government began calling up "old men" between twenty-five and thirty.

A group from South Philadelphia joined his unit, and they took a liking to him. On one occasion, they offered to beat up a guy for him because they thought he might be giving Henry a hard time. Henry told the South Philly guys that he could have taken the troublemaker, but it was good to know he had them on his side.

They would grab a guy who they thought was too proud late at night and give him a "scrub down" in the showers with soap and a few punches if they thought the guy was a problem. Those guys were real street toughs, but you could leave your wallet on your bed for the day, and it would still be there, money and all, when you got back.

Henry always admired their "old school code." *They had respect*, he thought, *like those boys from Cobbtown.*

Chapter 9

Postwar Energy

After the Fight of '47, the boys head over to the Tybee Pavilion. Folks are eating hot dogs and hamburgers, drinking sodas, enjoying hand-dipped ice cream cones, and a few pour whiskey into their cups. But all are happy and laughing as many dance to the big band sound led by a young trumpeter from Savannah named George Doener. The crowd roars and sings along when the band starts to play "The Boogie Woogie Bugle Boy" in honor of all vets. Lafayette grabs a girl by the hand, and they start dancing. Jack and Henry stand back, but Billy gets out and starts dancing with anyone and everyone. Several Savannah High School guys approach Lafayette and Billy, thanking them for lending them a hand.

"Didn't expect you Cadets to help, but you did. Thanks."

"It wasn't me. It was Butler and McGee," Billy explains, pointing to his buddies looking out at the dancers.

The band keeps playing, and the boys, girls, and older adults keep dancing. Cigarette and cigar smoke fill the air. Tybrisa is enjoying a new golden era—postwar energy. Tybee has come a long way since it had to dim the lights at night and paint the top half of the car headlights black to confuse any German U-boats from using the lights to navigate. In fact, if history is correct, there was a time when only one or two people lived on the Island—a bachelor lighthouse keeper and maybe a helper.

The nightlife virtually disappeared during the war years, but it's back stronger than ever. The band has fun as it starts to play "McNamara's Band," a top hit these days, and everyone joins in singing.

The war had come to Savannah just five years ago when a Savannah Line merchant ship, the SS City of Atlanta, was torpedoed off Cape Hatteras on January 19, 1942. Almost the entire crew was lost, except for three who held onto wreckage and were picked out from the cold waters of the Atlantic by another merchant marine vessel. Black and white, officer and enlisted, young and seasoned—there were only three survivors. It was really then that the war had come to Savannah, making a big impact on the community and awakening them to how close the European Theater could come if the Nazis weren't stopped. It seemed every able-bodied young man had tried to sign up. You'd never know it now as the music and lights are blaring and the crowds are singing happy tunes.

Billy suddenly starts singing, "Let it snow, let it snow, let it snow." People laugh and join in until the boys realize it is time to head back to the Lot. They walk and talk but eventually begin to sing again. This time, it is "Peg O' My Heart!"

"I've got to see the Peg O' My Heart soon," Henry says.

"Me, too," Jack remarks.

"I've got to make a phone call to ALL of my Pegs," Lafayette says.

"I have to find a Peg O' My Heart!" Billy adds, making the group burst out in laughter.

As the boys walk down the sandy road to the Lot, they see a fire blazing. Panicking, they surmise the house has caught fire from cinders. The closer they get, they realize it's just the wood-burning fire they had going at night to keep the bugs away. Phil Keane has finally shown up and is simply working by its light, apparently coming in late from Savannah.

"Keane, is that you?" Henry hollers.

"Well, it's not Robinson Crusoe. Henry, I told you I'd get here. I worked 'til after lunch in the lumberyard, went home, and had to run an errand for my folks. Then, I started hitching rides to Tybee. People were leaving the Island by then, but I managed to get here, as you can see," Keane explains. "I worked while it was still light and then got the fire going and worked some more, mostly straightening up. Grandpa came over to make sure I was part of the 'Savannah group,' then waited, knowing y'all were out drinking and doing God knows what else."

"Yeah, drinking and fighting—a few of us anyway," Jack says.

"Who, Adams and Burns?" Phil asks.

"Do you really need to ask?" Henry says.

"Just defending our honor," Lafayette says.

"And old High School," Jack adds.

"Glory, glory to old High School," Billy remarks.

"Let's get some sleep. Mass in the morning—late morning," one of the boys says.

"Amen," Billy answers.

Henry can't sleep very well. They're all lying on the floor of the hammock house now. The bugs keep getting through holes in his mosquito net, which he has set up between the house framing, which is still going up. He sees Jack near the fire and gets up to sit with him.

"Can't sleep either, heh?" Henry asks him.

"Nope, and you and I didn't even drink much," Jack notes.

"Things have changed a lot. Haven't they, Jack?" Henry asks.

"Yeah, that's what I've been thinking," Jack answers. "Things have changed, and we've changed just in a short time."

"I mean, I'm enjoying this, and I think you are too, Henry, but we have to move on. We're going off to school and gonna get married and have kids. It won't be like this anymore. Too much like high school," Jack notes.

"I don't want to be one of those guys who peak at seventeen or eighteen and is always going back reliving some dumb football game or teenage romance or something," Jack explains.

"You won't, Jack. You're too smart. We've got the GI Bill and will continue our education, get married, have families, and come to Tybee with our wives and the kids.

We'll make new memories," Henry says.

"Yeah," Jack replies.

"We have one more year at Armstrong, and we can hang out here on some weekends and breaks and then go from there," Henry adds. "It's been a great summer and will be another great year. It's like the Navy. Some guys hated it; we liked it. Served our country and met a lot of good guys."

Jack starts to smile and says, "I'll always remember going on report when you and I and that guy from Jacksonville Beach were sunning ourselves on the deck of that scuttled PT boat."

That pain in the neck ensign caught us and wrote me and 'Jacksonville Beach' up, but you had a little paintbrush in your hand and said you were painting the running lights on the PT boat and didn't pull KP!"

"That was funny," Henry says.

"For you!" Jack answers back.

"Or when the chief had too much to drink and was racing

around in a skiff in one of the inlets, and the lieutenant radioed me about the noise. I said, 'What racket, Lieutenant?'

He asked, 'How long have you been in the Navy, son?' I told him, 'Not long, sir." Then I forgot to let go of the button on the mike and..."

Henry starts to laugh, so Jack finishes for him, remembering the event. "And you said, 'Why? How long have YOU been in the Navy?"

Henry continues, "He went bananas and came running down, but you know, he ended up being a pretty good guy."

"Yeah, and you got off again," Jack says. "You did, Henry. And remember the other time you were sleeping in someone else's bunk, our favorite ensign showed up again, read the wrong name on the bunk, and wrote that person up."

"Yes, but that guy had been discharged, so I didn't feel bad," Henry replies. "Jack, you have a good memory for the breaks I got."

"I find you an interesting specimen, McGee," Jacks says, smiling. It's like you're charmed."

"No, I'm just lucky like you, and I make my Morning Offering every day like Sister Mary Margaret at Sacred Heart School taught us," Henry adds.

"O Jesus, through the Immaculate Heart of Mary, I offer You my prayers, works, joys and sufferings, all that this day may bring, be they good or bad, for the love of God, for the conversion of sinners, and in reparation for all the sins committed against the Sacred Heart and the Immaculate Heart of Mary."

"I'll have to start doing that again, Henry," Jack says, now laughing.

"You see, Jack, we have had some good times, even after high school, and we'll have more with the wives and kids one day if things work out. Not to mention engineering school for you and, hopefully, law school for me," Henry says.

"Henry, what kind of law are you going to practice?" Jack asks.

"I'm going to be a Navy JAG who defends enlisted guys who don't have a clue!"

The boys laugh.

"Let's hit the sack, Jack," Henry says.

Chapter 10

Sunday Best

The Savannah Boys sleep late and wash up in Grandpa's outdoor shower. They shave and change into white dress shirts, khaki pants, and thin neck ties they brought for church. Three leave in the DeSoto. Billy is running late but quickly catches a ride as he thumbs to St. Michael's. They join each other, sitting in the back of the church near the stained-glass window of Jesus Accepts His Cross and Jesus Dies on the Cross.

"The Fourth and Fifth Sorrowful Mysteries of the Rosary," Phil notes.

The priest walks out from the sacristy and begins the Prayers at the Foot of the Altar. Invoking St Michael the Archangel, he prays.

"Introibo ad altare Dei.
(I will go to the altar of God.)
Ad Deum qui laetivicat iuventutem meam.
(To God who giveth joy to my youth)

· · ·

"St. Michael the Archangel defend us in battle.
Be our safeguard against the wickedness and
snares of the Devil,
May God rebuke him,
We humbly pray
And do thou, Prince of the Heavenly Hosts, cast
into hell Satan and all evil spirits who prowl
about the earth seeking the ruin of souls."

A large statue of St. Michael the Archangel stands vigilant on the altar, its foot on the neck of a serpent representing the Devil. The angel is suited in armor and wields a sword, symbolizing the righteous archangel.

"Tossed him right out of Paradise, St. Michael did, Billy," Jack says.

"The strong arm of the law?" Billy asks.

"Yeah, the strong arm of the Lord," Jack answers.

Billy and Lafayette don't go to Communion. Phil Keane carries the rosary he has been saying during the whole Mass up with him when he kneels down at the altar rail to receive the Sacred Host and make his Holy Communion. Henry follows everything closely in the black missal his mother had given him when he was confirmed by the Bishop of Savannah at Sacred Heart Church some years ago. Father Ragan gives the final blessing and leaves through the sacristy again. The boys are sanctified for another week.

Father Ragan is known as "Fr. Hurricane" by locals. He is forever praying that storms and hurricanes will pass without claiming any lives or destroying everything in their path. True to form, at the end of Mass, Fr. Hurricane announces that hurricane season is here and prays accordingly.

Billy and Lafayette figure they need confession for the fight last night but decide they'll wait 'til they get back to Savannah and go one Saturday evening instead of bothering the priest before Mass this morning. They figure they are covered since they are sorry and intend to go to confession. However, they'll probably do the same if confronted with the same situation again. Guessing that's the sin of presumption, they decide they won't go to Communion. At least they won't go to hell for being dishonest, they reason. The boys live by the code, "Be true to yourself."

The sanctified souls get breakfast at a popular diner where the after-church crowd gathers. They eat eggs, bacon, toast, and grits, as well as plenty of coffee, cereal and milk for the kids, and the standard small glass of Florida orange juice.

After breakfast, the boys are all together again in Henry's DeSoto and decide to stop off at Memorial Park to join in a game of half-rubber. The park is behind the Tybee City Hall, an antebellum-looking one-story building. The park has recently been named after the many veterans from WWII who hailed from Tybee. It's amazing so many guys and girls volunteered and served from such a small community. Henry thinks there must have been a shortage of young adults at Tybee during the lean years of the war. *The good people of Tybee know the value of sacrifice, as so many left home to be part of the war effort. People from Tybee are truly "the salt of the earth,"* Henry concludes.

The game of half-rubber is simply a southern coastal version of northern stickball. It was "invented" in Pin Point, Georgia, a small fishing community founded by freed Blacks following the Civil War. It derives from a game played on the streets of Savannah and Charleston where city kids with broomsticks would hit bottle caps spun in the air. The game, despite its invisible base runners, can be surprisingly active. The pitcher is the key, and Henry is a natural at throwing the half-rubber disc across the hitting and strike zone. The Savannah boys are two up against the Island boys with two "base runners" on bases and an Island batter up with two outs. The rules are very flexible, so it's all or nothing at the top of this inning. The Island Boys are outstanding half-rubber players, and some play it for about ten months out of the year, off and on all day. The boys from Tybee are well-tanned and lean, wearing only their shorts. They contrast the Boys of Summer, who still wear their khakis and white shirts, although their shirts are unbuttoned and their ties have been removed.

"Sunday Best!" one of the members of the Tybee team calls them.

"Not a bad name for our team," remarks Phil Keane.

The Tybee boys prove they can swing a broomstick, field, and snag the odd-shaped "ball," which is liable to do anything and go anywhere once thrown or hit; thus, the fun and exercise of the game.

"Pitching, hitting, and fielding...no runners...that's the game of...half-rubber!" as the ditty goes.

Rules vary from neighborhood to neighborhood, region to region, and even game to game. Sportsmanship and a relaxed but competitive spirit are the soul of the game. Arguably, the best players are at Pin Point, a small fishing community near Skidaway Island outside of Savannah, followed by the Tybee-ites and then the boys from the City of Savannah, who are often from Tybee, too. The places have always overlapped, with many Savannahians spending long periods there and owning homes in Tybee and Savannah. The Savannah folks say Charlestonians are the least skilled, although Charleston players say the same about Savannah players. Occasionally, players meet up at Tybee or beaches like Sullivan's Island or the Isle of Palms near Charleston.

Henry throws a beautiful, perfect pitch to the batter. The disc-shaped rose-colored ball sails through the air and then slowly rises, almost stopping mid-air. The Tybee batter keeps his focus and a keen eye on the spinning and floating rose-colored ball. He looks up at it, steps back a little, and swings confidently, hitting the rubber and smashing it skyward to the fielder, Phil Keane. Phil runs back towards a little old cemetery overgrown with weeds and loses sight of it in the afternoon sun. The ball lands in the graveyard amongst a few grave markers and in the weeds. The Island boys win as all invisible runners are on the base, and the home run hitter crosses home plate. The winning team celebrates briefly, shakes hands with their opponents, and then scurries for a water break only to return to continue the southern coastal stickball game.

Henry turns and walks towards the cemetery. Phil is reading one of the tombstones, oblivious to the loss.

"Er, uh, Phil, are you there...Oh, Phil?" Henry half-jokingly asks.

"Yeah, I know we lost. I was just reading this marker," Phil says quietly, looking at an infant's little grave and marker.

"And the ball is lost," Henry reminds him.

"This child didn't live long," Phil reflects. "Just a few months."

"Bad Luck?" Henry asks.

"Maybe, but I'd like to think every life serves a purpose, no matter how short," Phil says. "And the markers on the ones over there say all three washed ashore in

1876. I wonder what ship they were on?"

"The SS Fate," Henry responds.

"Yeah, I guess, Henry. It was their fate."

"Say an Ave Maria, and let's blow this popsicle stand," Henry says, trying to get Phil grounded.

"I already said a prayer, Henry...I already prayed for all of their souls," Phil replies. "*Requiescat in pace.*" He adds, "You know, there's a marker on a grave at Catholic Cemetery in Savannah that says, 'Bend Thy knee for me and say an Ave Maria.'"

"No, can't say I ever read that one," Henry adds quietly.

"I read a lot of them," Phil says as he makes the sign of the cross and turns away.

The Savannah boys leave the cemetery and return to the Lot where they don't do much of anything except decide to head home and return early during the week. Besides, "No servile work on the Lord's Day!" Laf announces.

Significant progress has been made in just several days. Grandpa will look after things. "Re-group," as Lafayette says.

The boys pile into the DeSoto. Keane is with them this time, and they head back to Savannah and "civilization."

Billy Burns announces, "You know, going to Tybee is like leaving Savannah without leaving Savannah."

Henry surmises, "That's why I like it. Close to home, but far, far away." The other boys agree.

"I gotta work this week making gasoline deliveries. Won't be taking any day off, but I'll try to get down in the evenings if I can catch a ride and Henry comes back to town," Billy says. "Otherwise, it's a weekend deal."

"I'll be here," Lafayette announces.

"Same," Henry says.

"Me, too," Butler adds.

"I'll make a delivery during the week. Got some around the Island already," Keane says. "Let's move out," Henry commands.

The DeSoto heads west on US 80 back to Savannah, past Jake's, the fish camp at Lazaretto Creek, across the bridge, leaving Tybee for now.

"You know, if we kept going west, we would end up in..." Billy starts to say.

"Yeah, we know, San Diego," the other four boys answer almost together.

"People are going to start flying and driving more. My dad says the railroads are declining," Keane remarks.

"There will always be the rails, Phil," Henry says.

"Tell that to the Marsh Hen," Keane answers.

"Yeah, the Marsh Hen has gone to the railroad cemetery," Jack comments.

"Everything does, Jack," Henry adds.

"How about Gene Carney driving to the BC camp out on Coffee Bluff, missing a curve, and..." Billy paused.

"Gene was speeding, Billy, trying to get there in a hurry," Henry notes.

"Is that why you drive so slow, Henry?" Lafayette asks.

"Yeah, Lafayette, that's exactly why. Because of Gene and others we all know," Henry responds.

"Requiescat in pace," Jack Butler prays.

"Yeah, rest in peace, Gene," the boys pray as well.

"You know, Yankee gunboats patrolled these creeks and rivers during the Civil War," Phil Keane observes. "There are batteries all over where the Rebels would fire at them...my brother and I found musket balls and buttons from uniforms on a battery on Whitemarsh Island. Arrowheads and shark teeth, too, all over the place. I got a cigar box full of stuff like that."

"One day, there will be houses out here, and all that will be bulldozed over," Lafayette says.

"No one wants to live out here, but a few Island people who fish and do odd jobs. Nothing out here, and the mosquitos are huge," Keane says.

"Better collect your bullets and buttons now, Phil. I think Lafayette is right," Henry says.

"These islands are too low, Henry. Who would build a house out here besides fishermen? When the first hurricane hits at high tide, it's 'Hello, Atlantic Ocean.' That's why they all have boats sitting in their front yards. Ever notice that?" Keane asks.

Henry drops off Billy and Lafayette on the east side and Keane near Blessed Sacrament Church, a white clapboard church at the corner of Victory and Waters.

Jack points to the building. "Did you know they're getting ready to build a new church and school?"

"Yeah, I know. I pledged $50. We used to go there until we moved into Sacred Heart," Henry notes.

"Someone called on me for a pledge. I told them I went to the Cathedral and Monsignor McNamara wouldn't be too keen if I pledged to them," Butler says.

"Say, Jack, you mind if I ride by Margaret Conner's house?" Henry asks.

"Go ahead. I know you like her," Jack kindly says.

"Yeah, and it won't look as weird if you're with me," Henry responds. "Thanks, Jack."

"I know what you mean. I like Billy's younger sister, Helen, and I'd like to ask her out, but I don't want to be riding by Billy's house. He'd start giving me a hard time. I'll have to wait to run into her after Mass," Jack says. "Plus, her mother doesn't like me. Says there are too many boys in my family! I say all the more reason to let me go out with Helen. I've got brothers who will watch out for her."

"You told her that?" Henry asks.

"No, but I will..." Jack responds.

Henry rides by the stately home at Atlantic and 40th near the park.

"The Conners are seafaring people, three generations of

maritime officers, and they dabble in real estate as well," Jack observes.

"She's popular with the 'lace curtain Irish' guys who go to Sacred Heart, Henry," Jack says.

"Like me, Jack?" Henry asks, smiling.

"Oh, yeah, like you and me, Henry!" Jack responds.

As the black DeSoto cruises by Margaret's house, Henry casually glances over at the driveway and notices a car missing.

"She must be out in her brother's car again. It figures," Henry says.

"Why don't you stop here, go up to the door, and knock on it to make sure?" Jack asks jokingly.

"Let me get you home, Jack," Henry adds.

"No, why don't you circle around the block ten times, Henry?" Jack says, laughing this time.

"Yeah, right. Have her mother call my mother," Henry responds. "No thanks. Next time, you can walk back from the beach, Jack."

Jack just laughs, and Henry begins to laugh with him. Jack slaps Henry lightly on his shoulder with his left hand and says, "Home, Henry!"

"We are home, Jack. Thanks be to God! We are home!"

Chapter 11

Happy Tears

Henry's mom and dad are getting ready for Sunday dinner when he walks in the door. He's still wearing his dress shirt and pants with his tie hanging down. He apologizes before his mother says anything, washes up, pulls his tie up, sits with his parents, and then crosses himself and offers grace.

"I'm glad you went to Mass, Henry," his mother says.

"He better," his father adds.

"He does, Lawrence," his mother says to her husband.

"Always, Dad, just like you and Mom and the nuns taught me," Henry says.

"And the priests, Henry," his mother adds.

"And the priests and the brothers and the Lord..." Henry says.

"That's enough, Henry," his father warns him.

"Sorry, Mother and Dad," Henry says.

"I saw the Conner girl's mother today at the bookstore," Henry's mom comments.

"Oh yeah?" Henry answers.

"And she is such a nice lady, very elegant, like her daughter. Margaret, I think her name is," his mother continues. "Do you know her, Henry?"

"Of course, Mother, she was in my class at Sacred Heart," Henry answers. "You meet a lot of nice people volunteering at the Catholic bookstore, don't you, Mother?"

"Lots," Mary St. John responds.

"Too many," Mr. McGee says.

"You can never meet too many people, Lawrence," his wife responds.

"How's the house coming along, son?" Mr. McGee asks, changing the topic.

"Hey, Dad, it's great!" Henry responds. "Jack, Laf, Billy, and Phil are there."

"They're good friends, "Henry's dad observes, "and that project is a good experience for all of you."

"Yes, sir, I'm lucky," Henry answers.

The dinner consists of roast beef, mashed potatoes, gravy, sweet peas, and peach cobbler pie. It's a grand Sunday dinner, a little heavy in the heat, but Mom's good ole' southern cooking."

"I'll take a walk after dinner," Henry's dad says, "and then hit the sack."

"Have you heard from Karl?" Henry asks.

"A letter came Friday. I forgot to tell you, but he's doing wonderful. He thinks he's passed all of his tests and can keep his commission!" Mrs. McGee responds.

"That's great! Karl deserves it," Henry observes.

"Of course he does, Henry. He's a war hero!" his mother exclaims.

"He sure is Mother and Dad. He sure is," Henry answers.

"I just don't know about him staying in...We live in perilous times," Mother remarks.

"We always live in perilous times, Mary. He has an opportunity to stay in and get promoted and maybe retire a senior officer," Henry's dad adds.

"And he's dating a lovely girl named Susan," Mrs. McGee remarks. "I asked Karl if she was..." She pauses mid-sentence, makes the Sign of the Cross as if the gesture flowed fluently in conversation, and finishes her sentence, "and he said she was! But he wouldn't tell me her background, though. Irish? English? Italian? Makes me wonder."

"She's Japanese American," Henry blurts out, "and he really loves her!"

"Oh...er...well...I wished he'd have told us..." Mrs. McGee says.

"He asked me to tell you," Henry says.

"Oh, I see. She's Catholic, though?" Mrs. McGee asks.

"Very Catholic, Mother," Henry says.

Mr. McGee sits there, taking it all in. "Help your mother with the dishes, son, and bring me a shot of Old Grand Dad. I'm going to drink to my son and this Susan. Henry, I'm proud of both of them." He smiles, gets up, lights a cigarette, and gets ready to walk outside.

"All three, Lawrence? His wife asks, now focusing a little on her youngest son, Henry.

"All four—Karl and Susan, Henry, and you, most of all, Mary St. John," he says playfully, calling her by her maiden name.

"Henry, make that a double," he commands.

"Yes, sir," Henry says.

"And pour your mother one, too," he smiles again.

"Japanese, you say, Henry?" His mother asks.

"Japanese and American and Catholic," Henry responds.

Henry's mother begins to cry.

"Are those happy tears or sad ones, Dad?" Henry asks his father.

"I think they're all three, son," his dad says.

"All three?" Henry asks.

"Yeah, happy, sad, and mother tears. Now don't ask me anything else. Get those drinks and make sure you finish what you started at Tybee," he says.

"Oh...yes, sir," Henry responds.

Chapter 12

Forsyth Park

I t's early one evening, and Jack Butler and Henry McGee are back in Savannah. Although the DeSoto is broken down, they walk to the Knights of Columbus Hall on Liberty and Bull. Henry and Jack climb the large wooden staircase to the upstairs floor after ordering two bottled beers at the bar on the first floor of the council building, which is built up one story from Liberty Street with little stores below it. There are several billiard tables and a rack of pool sticks upstairs.

"Choose your weapon and rack 'em up, McGee," Butler calls out.

Several other men play at the table next to theirs. One man is dressed in an untucked, short-sleeved, red plaid shirt with khakis and white sneakers. The other man is

dressed in a white T-shirt with a pack of cigarettes rolled up in one of the sleeves. His shirt is tucked into his blue work jeans, held up by a dark brown belt.

The cuffs of his jeans are neatly folded up just enough to show his white socks and ox-blood-colored loafers. He has slicked-back dark brown hair. A cigarette dangles from his mouth.

"Heard you and McGee got into a fight with some 'crackers' at Tybee, Butler," the man in the untucked plaid shirt says as he watches his partner line up a shot.

"It was Burns and Adams," Butler replies. "It's always Burns and Adams…"

"Yeah, we know," the man with the slicked-back hair says with a smirk as he shoots a shot and pockets a ball. "They're both still fighting the war."

"Which war?" McGee asks.

"The Revolution, the War Between the States, the Spanish-American War," the man replies, still smirking.

"All of them," Butler says.

"Yeah, ALL of them," the man responds as he misses his next shot.

The plaid-shirt man asks, "You fellas going to invite us down to the retreat house when it's finished?"

"Yeah, after Father Damien puts the 'ergo te' on it," Butler responds.

"You better batten it down. A few tropical storms are developing in Florida, one big one in Cape Sable," the plaid-shirt man advises as the game continues.

"They don't come to Savannah or Tybee too often, far too west from the Continental Shelf…" Butler says.

"Murphy's Law is alive and well, Butler and McGee, 'If anything can go wrong, it will,'" the man responds as he takes a shot and knocks the 8 ball into one of the holes. "You see. Scratch," he says, throwing the stick on the table.

The men play an hour or so more, and Butler and McGee walk out of the council hall and down Bull towards the Big Park, leaving the other two men in the room.

"There's a shrimp boil later here, Henry; we could stick around," Jack suggests.

"Nothing like Tybee Island shrimp—best in the world, some say," Jack says. "It has that wild ocean taste with a little sweetness," Jack adds.

"Naw, I have stuff I gotta do at home, Jack," Henry answers.

"Margaret?" Jack asks, smiling.

"Maybe," Henry responds with a smirk.

"Why don't you ask her to the shrimp boil?" Jack says.

"Would be too late without the DeSoto, Jack," Henry says.

"Have her drive you there in her brother's car, Henry," Jack says, almost laughing.

"Yeah, right, Butler," Henry responds.

"Besides, all the guys will be there drinking beer and talking loud," Henry notes. "Well, that's a shrimp boil, McGee." Jack gets the last word in. "A shrimp boil is tamer than one of those oyster roasts outside in the winter with the fire going and the whiskey flowing."

I guess... let's go home, Jack," Henry says.

"I think those guys are right, Jack. We need to put siding on that house and batten it down somehow. Keane can get the rest of the stuff. We can get the cash."

"You're too cautious, Henry. It's a risk. Anything like that is, but you're right. I'd like to enjoy it a while before we leave town. You know Billy will be working more delivering gas. Laf will join up again, and hopefully, you and I will graduate and go off to finish four years of college," Butler notes.

The young men continue to talk about their future as they stroll down Bull Street past antebellum homes, historic buildings, houses of worship, and through the squares, past Sergeant William Jasper, an American Revolutionary hero. Henry glances over to his right and recalls that the rectory of St. John's

Episcopal Church was once headquarters to General William Tecumseh Sherman after he completed his infamous March to the Sea and captured the City of Savannah. In December 1864, he presented it to President Lincoln as a Christmas gift.

Jack Butler recalls a family story of Sherman's occupation of Savannah when he tells Henry that he had a distant relative working in a German bakery that once operated behind St. John's Church. When Sherman's army came into the city and was marching down Bay Street, some of the help hid in the large flour barrels of the day. They were coaxed out hours later, covered in white flour.

"It must have been a sight, Henry," Jack quips.

The boys then pass the statue of Casimir Pulaski, another American Revolutionary.

"Where's Oglethorpe's statue?" Jack asks.

"Two heroes back," Henry answers.

"Was he a hero too?" Jack asks.

"Sort of a hero. Founder of Savannah," Henry guesses.

"Lots of heroes, Henry," Jack comments. "Like Karl," he adds.

"Thanks, pal," Henry responds.

"You're welcome, Henry," Jack says, smiling.

They continue past what they hope will be their alma mater, Armstrong Junior College. They reach Gaston Street, where Jack heads east to his home, and Henry walks through the Big Park down the wide sidewalk that runs right down the middle, past the big fountain.

A cop on the beat, dressed in his light blue long-sleeve shirt with dark pants and wearing a black tie, eight-point cap, and Sam Brown belt, opens one of the police call boxes in the Big Park he patrols. An easy beat as there was rarely a crime committed in the park—even late at night. Henry sees several couples holding hands and hopes he and Margaret can one day soon take a stroll in the park amongst the live oaks and azaleas. *Women love that. In fact, I'd like that, too*, he thinks.

Forsyth Park, or the Big Park, is a thirty-acre public park bounded by Drayton and Whitaker Streets on the east and west and Gaston and Park Streets on the north and south. Near the center of the park is "The Fountain," designed after one in Paris. It soothes the spirits of many visitors with its comforting water sounds.

The neighborhood changes from colonial and antebellum homes to Victorian houses with detailed woodwork and open verandas where hanging baskets are placed, matching the greenery of the surrounding gardens and the park. Several homes appear on either side of the park, like medieval castles with Victorian domed turrets in the distance, facing the lush semi-tropical gardens.

Henry walks around the Confederate Memorial and reaches the end of the park, where a larger-than-life figure of a soldier of the Spanish-American War monument stands with his Krag Carbine rifle, looking south down Bull Street, ever vigilant.

The sentry "greeted" the BC Cadets as they marched north down Bull Street from Benedictine Military School to drill in Forsyth Park during the weekdays, stopping traffic in all directions. The Cadets drilled where Confederate and later Union soldiers once camped, and Billy once kicked up a Union button from what he guessed was one of Sherman's soldiers as he marched in the grassy field. He replaced one of the missing buttons on his dress grey uniform with it as sort of a war trophy until the retired Army colonel who headed the Corps of Cadets noticed it and "confiscated" it, adding it to his Civil War button collection. Billy was given two demerits for being out of uniform, but the colonel thanked him for the button.

Henry continues south towards BC. He passes the

Chatham Artillery Building, where the big band sound comes from the second-floor dance floor. People in formal dress laugh and talk loudly as they leave their parked cars and enter the building. He passes the yellow brick Sears Building and crosses Anderson and Henry Streets near Bull Street Baptist, the Greek Orthodox Church, and St. Paul's Lutheran Church.

"Church row," his dad calls it. To some of the old timers, Henry recalls, this is the southernmost boundary of the City. Jerry George's Soda Fountain is nearby on Bull Street and is getting ready to close for the evening. He remembers gathering there after school and, on an occasional Saturday, drinking chocolate malts. A sweet roll covered in thick white frosting from Gottlieb's across from the soda shop was a real treat, too.

He crosses himself as he passes Sacred Heart Catholic Church. A few of the old Benedictine monks in their black robes are sitting in rocking chairs on the big porch of the priory next to the church. One smokes a cigar that Henry can smell from across the street. He glances over at his old high school, where the gym door is open, and the high school kids are playing basketball. A few are on the outside, "horsing around."

The gym is designed after a similar building at West Point and called "The Armory." Calling the gym an armory always seemed a bit of a misnomer to Henry since it was where the Cadets mostly played basketball more than where they planned for another northern invasion of Savannah. Henry even had a little office on the second floor where he worked on the high school newspaper, the Campus Quill, and wrote the column "I'll BCing You." Henry thinks to himself as he passes his old high school. *I'll be seeing you. That was me about three years ago, "Tempus fugit," and it sure does seem so long ago. I guess because a lot has happened, he thinks to himself, and I pray good things will continue to happen...*

As Henry goes further south past the public library and crosses 37th Street, he turns east on 40th Street near the Starland Dairy building to go home.   He figures he'll keep walking east towards Baldwin Park down 40th Street to Margaret Conner's house. Henry McGee laughs to himself. *I just need more exercise and fresh air. And might as well walk by Peg O' My Heart's house. I mean, she may come running out and leap into my arms!* He laughs again and goes east, right by his own house, towards Margaret Conner's whispering and singing,

> *"Peg O' My Heart!*
> *I love ya,*
> *Don't let us part, I love you.*
> *I always knew*
> *It would be you*
> *Since I heard your lilting laughter*
> *It's your Irish heart I'm after*
> *Peg O' My Heart..."*

Henry thinks that if the boys could hear him, they'd sock him one. Just then, one of Henry's neighbors, an old man named Mr. Sapp, hollers from his porch, "Henry, for the sake of the neighborhood, can you please take some voice lessons!"

Henry turns and says, "Oh, hello, Mr. Sapp. You certainly hear well."

"Well, Henry, listening to you ruin that good song. I wished I didn't!" Mr. Sapp says, chuckling.

"I'll take those voice lessons," Henry responds.

"Lonely old man," Henry mutters to himself.

"What was that, Henry?" Old Man Sapp calls out.

"I just said, lonely night for a young man, Mr. Sapp," Henry responds.

"Well, why don't you ask that Conner girl out? That's where you're heading, isn't it?" Mr. Sapp asks, chuckling.

"Got to finish my walk, Mr. Sapp. See ya!" Henry responds.

"See ya, young feller, and thanks for your service!" Mr. Sapp yells. "You've earned the right to sing aloud."

Now he wants me to sing, Henry thinks to himself...*and after all of that.*

"Thank you, Mr. Sapp," Henry responds.

"Don't let us part! Da da da da, da da da da..."

Henry McGee walks past the Conner house, then turns around at the park and walks by the Conner house again, singing and glancing momentarily at the home of Margaret Conner. He walks around the corner to 41st Street, wanting to avoid Mr. Sapp and his unsolicited advice, then heads home. Entering his back door into the kitchen, he makes a navy bean sandwich and pours a big glass of cold milk. *I'm like Perry Como says, a prisoner of love. Building that beach house is easy compared to this "prison,"* he laughs to himself...

It's back to Tybee ASAP to "finish what he started."

Chapter 13

Tybee Sunsets

Henry is up early, like a Marine. He hears only what he guesses to be a nightingale. Even the up-before-morning larks are asleep. Henry will be by himself on this drive to Tybee. The others will somehow join him later. This morning is somewhat cooler than it's been as Henry moves east on Victory Drive and then Tybee Road in the DeSoto with its windows open and the cooler air coming in through the side vent windows and hitting him through the driver and passenger's side. He'll get there first and just start hammering or cleaning or something. Like his dad would command him when Henry sat idle, "Make yourself useful, son."

There is hardly a car on the road that is not going towards the Island. Henry takes time to reflect as he drives this cool summer morning, where a Tybee marsh mist has settled once again. Henry feels lucky this morning. He is determined to ask Margaret out, is going to college on the GI Bill, and is building a house at Tybee. He has good friends who are tried and true.

Loyalty is important to Henry. He recalls a loyalty poem that ends with a warning for those who lack this quality: "The first strong wind will come along and blow you away, and you will never know why." The Boys of the Summer of 1947 are loyal friends.

There's Jack Butler, who is not only a gridiron star but also an excellent student. He possesses natural leadership abilities, a type of charisma that one is simply born with. He and Henry are rivals but will stand together in tough times.

Billy Burns is a comedian who was the first to help a friend. Phil Keane is a sensitive artist and warrior poet. Henry surmises that Phil is not made for this world, but he always comes through when the seas get rough.

Yes, some people aren't made for this world, Henry thinks, but he believes everyone has a purpose and that everything works toward the common good.

Finally, Lafayette Adams. His name explains it all! Henry remembers hearing in a high school history class that an aide to General Pershing, as American doughboys arrived in France during WWI, exclaimed, "Lafayette, we are here!" honoring the Frenchman who, as an aristocrat and a French military offi-cer, came to America's assistance in the Revolutionary War. Mostly brawn, Lafayette Adams might not have been an officer and a gentleman, but he knew how to lead men in battle and would assist a friend in need just like his namesake. Lafayette Adams is impetuous, but his friends could always depend on him to back them up.

And me? Henry smiles to himself. He was close to his Grandfather McGee.

Granddaddy was Irish to the core of his being. In true immigrant style, he clawed his way to the top and became an honest, hardworking railroad executive. The rails and, later, his coveted position took their toll, and for a long time, Grand-daddy drank too much.

Life was hard for Irish immigrants then, and it is still the same for new groups arriving in America. The Irish, however, were a charitable lot. Henry's grandfather was kind to the underdog and taught his son and grandson to be the same. Henry remembers finding his grandfather passed out in front of the family home on Lincoln and Maupas, having come home early one morning after an all-night binger. Grandfather McGee made it to the house's front porch but not inside. Henry proceeded to rescue him by picking his grandfather up and bringing him into the bedroom Henry's father had given his dad after he became a widower. Henry would bring his grandfather coffee to bed after he awoke from his few hours of sleep, and his grandfather would not say anything except, "Thank you."

That "thank you" from his grandfather was enough for Henry, who simply sat there and watched his grandfather come to his senses again, happy to assist him. Henry figures he learned responsibility from his not-so-pleasant experiences with his grandfather and the importance of helping others. In other words, Henry is often his brother's keeper.

Henry always felt good when he was able to help his grandfather and alleviate his father and mother from having to worry about one more thing. Besides, Henry's father had probably done the same thing and was getting old and tired himself. Granddaddy was a tough Irishman, though, and one day, he went into sobriety and stayed on it until he passed away some years later. Henry figures something rattled him one day into a moment of sanity, and he "took the oath," and this time, he kept it.

Maybe it was Henry's mother's prayers...

Henry thought the booze might have already done its damage, though, as Granddaddy became senile and somewhat unpredictable, but he may have ended up like that anyway. Henry had learned a lot about heavy drinkers from a Navy chief while he and Jack served in the US Navy. This particular chief had given up the sauce years earlier when he almost killed another young sailor in a fight. He explained to Henry that children and even grandchildren of drunks often want to be in control of situations because they felt so out of control when those close to them were drinking heavily. The chief, who seemed to know about such things, further explained that those close to heavy drinkers could be controlling or the other extreme, one or the other. Henry liked following the rules and was generally content to do so. Henry guessed this quality had served him well and sparked his interest in the law.

He likes looking after his family and friends and always tries to give sound advice. He hopes to continue helping others, especially the underdogs, and offering good legal counsel. For now, however, Henry is enjoying Tybee and his friends.

Henry reaches the last bend in the highway before the Lazaretto Creek Bridge, the bridge to Tybee. "Where Ocean Breezes Blow," Henry whispers to himself, quoting the old Central of Georgia advertisement for the now defunct train rides from Savannah to Tybee. And "Where the Georgia 'Peaches' Go," Henry also whispers, remembering the title of the song by Samuel B. Miller and played by Dewey Holm and His Savannahians back in the '20s. *Bet the Tybrisa Pavilion was flapping in those days,* Henry thinks, smiling.

Henry recalls a stanza of the old song his parents danced to...

"Let us sing of Georgia beaches,
And those lovely Georgia peaches,
Down at Tybee."

As Henry rounds the final bend before the creek, he enters the bridge's narrow roadway, which seems to swallow him and his DeSoto whole this morning. The darkness envelops him, and he looks through the bridge's trusses onto the horizon, barely visible. The water is dark, almost black. "Ominous" is the word that comes to Henry's mind as he feels a real foreboding. He is relieved as he reaches the other side and exits the bridge back on the highway, passing the shrimp boats moored at the pier of the little fishing village. He motors faster now and turns down the sandy road to the Lot. This morning, Henry feels, for himself anyway, that the bridge he just crossed is the Bridge to Everywhere."

Yes, he is lucky, Henry concludes.

Henry notices Phil Keane's pickup truck already there but does not see "Phil the Lumberman." The old man is up before dawn, so Henry knocks on the door of the "marsh shack," hoping Grandpa might have seen Phil. Grandpa answers, dressed in his usual work khaki shirt and pants.

"Hello, Grandpa. Henry here."

"Yes, of course, 'Henry here.' What is such a young fellow like you up so early?" Grandpa asks, smiling as usual. "Coffee, young feller?"

"No, thank you. I was wondering if you saw Phil this morning?" Henry asks.

"Sure did. Said he was heading over to Fort Screven. You know, where the old back gate used to be, to watch the sunrise," Grandpa answers. "He seems like a good boy, but he sorta has his head in the clouds, you know?"

"Hey, thanks, Grandpa," Henry says as he starts down the dirt road toward Fort Screven and the beach.

"Come by for coffee later and bring the poet with you, Henry!" the old man hollers out.

Henry is a little worried, thinking Phil might take a solo swim. He guesses the sharks are out at night until early morning feeding. Not many shark attacks here, though. Henry surmises they must secretly drop oil bombs offshore to drive away the sharks like they do at Hilton Head.

The tide's moving out. Henry doesn't want Phil being yanked out to sea if he decides to take a swim.

Sure enough, Phil is sitting on a piece of driftwood, looking at the horizon.

"Lumberman!" Henry calls out.

"It's the Henry attack!" Phil responds. "Hello, Henry, guess Grandpa told you..."

"Of course, just glad you told someone since you're by yourself," Henry says as he sits down with his buddy.

"You should have been here a little earlier, Henry. That sunrise was something else," Phil observes. "A real burst of light and color. And then a ship coming out of the North Channel appeared in the foreground."

"Yeah, guess I don't watch too many sunrises or ships going out to sea, not like I could anyway," Henry notes.

"Lots of hues of orange and red," Phil observes.

Henry remarks, "Red sky in the morning sailors take warning."

"Guess they're ignoring the warning because they need to eat," Phil smiles as a small fishing boat appears in the foreground. Its shadowy outline becomes clearer with each passing moment and then navigates seaward and disappears into the horizon. "Spectacular!"

Henry thinks back to the boat he acquired as a young boy when he offered to buy an abandoned blue wooden boat on the shore of the south end of Sullivan's Island. It was half-buried in the sand and had once had an outboard attached to its strengthened stern. It had a partially covered bow for storage, and the back siding flared out somewhat to give it a sportier and more unique appearance. It was painted a light-colored blue, most of which had worn off as it sat in the salt air and sun on the narrow beach.

Henry guessed where the owner's home was and remembers going to the back screen porch where an old man was. When Henry asked the old man whether he'd be willing to sell the abandoned skiff and how much he wanted for it, the old man said, "You can have it, sonny!"

Henry could hardly believe his ears. "I can have it, sir?" Henry exclaimed.

"Yes, you can have it!" the man said again.

"Oh, thank you so much, sir!"

As he turned to run home and tell his brother, Karl, that he got a boat, the old man's wife could be heard yelling, "Now don't go taking that thing out into the harbor and drowning! You tell him now, don't go out and capsize it or let it sink!"

Henry took off. He didn't want to hear the old man tell him, "You better not have it, sonny. It might sink!"

Henry spent the day and the next trying to dig the boat out of the sand and then discovered it hadn't a bottom. It had rotted due to the dampness in the ground. *If only I had gotten there sooner,* he remembers thinking. *If only I had seen it sooner and asked the old man then.*

That was his first boat, and it never left port—not with him in it. He returned sometime later after a hurricane to see the boat gone. He guessed the boat was more than likely carried out to the ocean and laid to rest with a proper burial at sea.

Through the years, Henry discovered that things happen for a reason. He surmised that if the boat had any kind of bottom left, he would have launched it into the harbor, and it would have taken on water, been carried off by a current, sunk, and the boat and himself laid to rest with a burial at sea!

Glancing back to the sunrise, he says, "You ought to paint a Tybee sunrise and put a ship in it. You could add some marsh birds flying around or write about it or both, Phil. You're so talented."

"Thanks, Henry. I need a lot of encouragement, but I think I will. Thanks for the compliment; it's really nice of you," Phil says, shaking his head and glancing back at the horizon.

"Okay, buddy, but for now, let's get that beach house built, and you can sit on that back porch we're going to add and paint marsh scenes. I think you can see the sunset over there. Hadn't paid much attention to it, but thanks to you, I will now," Henry says.

"Well, thanks to you, I'll paint it, Henry," Phil answers.

The Boys of Summer, now turning to fall, get up from the driftwood chair and walk whimsically away from the ocean back towards the marshes and creeks near the Back River.

"Do you think pirates buried treasure on Tybee, Henry?" Phil asks as they make their way through the soft sand.

"I don't know whether they buried treasure or not, but my guess is they buried a lot of other things that just need to stay buried," responds Henry.

"Yeah, best not to go there..." Phil responds.

"But hey, you're a writer, too. It's okay to imagine those things and write about them!" Henry exclaims.

Chapter 14

Southerners

The boys did their best to follow the plans that Phil Keane's dad, who worked for the Corps of Engineers, had drawn up and had approved by the Corps. The building was nothing fancy; it was essentially a large room with a divider for the living area and bedroom. Plans included a kitchenette, a place for a cooler with block ice, a sterno-type stove, and a pantry. A well and a dock to run from the back porch to the creek will be dug later.

No power lines run to the hammock; gas lanterns are used. The "bathroom" is a camp-style field latrine at the far end of the hammock. Plans for a septic tank and an oil heater are pending. Contact with Grandpa has paid off, as he has an outdoor shower like many of the Tybee houses for returning beachgoers.

The idea is to spend a few days at a time on Tybee. The boys will fish and crab, go to the beach, eat out, build a fire at night, drink beer, and keep working on the house to make it more habitable.

"Roughing it," the boys tell one another. "This place is a

break from daily showering and shaving, gives us good shelter, a view of the marsh and creek, and the smell of the salt air." It's all the young vets desire.

Unfortunately, the construction started late. By the time the plans were drawn up, the land was found and purchased, permits were obtained, and agreements were made, summer was mostly over, and they were way over budget.

The group begins doing odd jobs on the Island to help make some extra money.

One afternoon, they offer to clean the underneath of houses. They guess the houses could use it, and the owners might have money to pay them for cleaning. One home was over one hundred years old and faced the ocean near the north end of the Island. It was built off the ground on huge round posts and was painted the traditional white with dark green shutters, which were used for storms and later for the offseason when not in use. It had two peaked sections, one on either side, and a flat roof section in the middle. Porches sat on the oceanside and the entrance. There were high ceilings and no hallways inside, just rooms that ran together from what the boys see as they talk to the owner, whose family has lived in the same house since before the Civil War.

The downstairs was classic Tybee with vertical siding that was spaced to let the breeze into the open space underneath the main living area. There was a dirt floor, an old fireplace no longer in use, an open gathering space, and what appeared to have been two other bedrooms for children or guests. An old brick cistern that arched into a half dome still caught rainwater. It looked more like one of the vaults in Colonial Cemetery in Savannah than something that collected rainwater for the household.

"Don't stand on the brick cistern," Henry barks. "It will collapse, and you will never be heard from again."

The boys obediently respond and then move onto the large porch, talking about the Union officers who most likely had slept in its bedrooms and had formal sit-down dinners in its dining room.

"Then the soldiers would sit on this porch facing the ocean and think of home as they smoked their cigars and sipped on their brandy. Servants would run over from the separate kitchen on the property waiting on 'the invaders' who were simply following orders from their superiors who had occupied the Island building earthworks on the north end to bombard Fort Pulaski," Laf explains.

The fort was a magnificently designed brick fortification built years ago at the mouth of the Savannah River to protect the waterway to the Port of Savannah.

"Hey, I bet you don't know the name of the officer who designed the moat system that surrounded the fort?" Billy asks.

The young men answer in unison, "Robert E. Lee." They all laugh that they know their history so well.

However, the demise of the old brick fort was inevitable with the invention of the rifled cannon, which fired missiles further and more intensely. Little did these men who had occupied the Island from up north know that they would be attacking their own fort one day, which would be occupied by other Americans.

To the southerners, however, the Yankee soldiers were the invaders and the enemy that their duty told them they must defend against. To the North, the southerners were the rebels they had to defeat and suppress until they capitulated and ceased their uprising. The rebellious southerners must, in other words, "Be squelched."

"I would have fought for my country, which was Georgia back then," declares Lafayette as the boys move old furniture out from underneath the house. The old man who owns it decides what to keep and what to burn.

"Georgia is not a country," responds Jack.

"It was back then, Jack," Laf answers.

"No more," Jack says, "just a state."

"Yeah, but that's not how they thought a hundred years ago," Laf responds.

"Well, we do now… they won, we lost," Jack adds.

"Oh, so you admit it!" Laf says.

"Admit what?" Jack asks.

"You admit that we lost, and they won! So there is an us and a them," Laf continues, pulling Jack's chain.

"There's always an us and a them, Laf," Jack responds.

"Okay then?" Laf says.

"Whatever," Jack quips.

As the boys clean out one of the rooms, they discover a door that opens to a back staircase. *There is always a back staircase in these old houses—for the kids and the help,* Henry remembers.

It is dark and even somewhat cooler underneath the house compared to the outside. There are strange-looking insects in the damp dirt and on the dusty floor of one of the rooms, which still has a floor. The little creatures wiggle and crawl away as the boys move the furniture they guessed had been there since the Civil War.

"Never really knew what musty smelled like until now," Laf quips.

"I wonder how this house looked and smelled when it was first built and if the downstairs was completely covered with flooring. I bet it once had fresh lumber, fresh paint, and fresh ocean air smell," Henry murmurs. He imagines families just like his coming in from the beach and rinsing off at a pump or something before changing into formal clothing and going upstairs for dinner.

They all marvel at the amount of lumber, old square-head nails, and wooden pegs that had held this old retreat house together for so long. Lots of cutting and sawing and hammering and just plain guessing back then, Henry observes. Not everything seemed square, but the house had settled into the sand foundation and withstood hundreds of squalls and a few hurricanes throughout the century. It's a worthy structure, Henry concludes, and filled with worthless dried-out junk that is musty and filled with more salt from the air than memories.

"Man, this would make great kindling for the bonfire at Bull and Broughton," Billy suggests.

The annual high school football game between Savannah High School and BC was played every Thanksgiving at Grayson Stadium. Thousands of people showed up to root for their alma mater, Old High School or BC. The game was intense but a friendly rivalry between a large public high school and a small parochial one.

Savannah High has a bigger team and better equipment, but both teams were known to be tough, and anything could happen as the emotions ran high. That's one thing that made the game so exciting and entertaining—it was simply unpredictable. Oftentimes, David slew Goliath, with BC coming out on top.

After the game, a gathering at Bull and Broughton was held, and a bonfire was lit in the nearby square. The winning team carried the coffin of the losing team. The fire department and Savannah police stood by. All went well despite a few fights that ended with a black eye, bloody nose, and handshake between the fighters.

Henry recalls how the worst thing that ever really happened was when some real hooligans ("criminal felons," the

DA called them) cut the firehoses. The fire could then burn bigger and hotter, which was pretty dumb considering it could have sent the whole of downtown burning to the ground.

Henry thinks the bonfire is ridiculous, but it serves a purpose by eliminating all the junk downtown and allowing young adolescents and frustrated athletes to vent.

Somehow, he knew it would never be that way again for him and his friends.

Chapter 15

Arranged by Angels

Without driving himself crazy about what to say, Henry simply picks up the phone and calls Margaret Conner's house. His prayers are answered when Margaret answers, not her mother or brother.

"Hello, Conner's residence, Margaret speaking."

"Oh, yes, Conner residence. I mean, oh yes, Margaret, this is Henry McGee."

"Hello, Henry," Margaret answers.

A promising sign, Henry thinks to himself. *She didn't hang up.*

"Yes, hello Margaret. I was wondering if..." Henry pauses.

"You were wondering what, Henry?" Margaret asks.

"I was wondering if you'd go out with me and Jack Butler and Helen Burns to the beach and then Harris's later...?"

"Yes, Henry, I'd like that!" Margaret answers happily.

"Hey..., oh, that's great!" Henry says.

"I'll pick you up at your house this Saturday around 10 a.m., okay?"

"Yes, that's fine," Margaret says.

"See you Saturday at 1000 hours," Henry adds.

Henry is so excited that he hangs up the phone with a bang and then hopes she hasn't heard it.

Henry remembers when he was a freshman in high school and still a scout in Troop 15 at Blessed Sacrament Church on Victory Drive. At one scout meeting, he volunteered to help the Sisters of Mercy clean their Grotto in the courtyard of the Mercy convent on Liberty and Abercorn. Henry's mother naturally thought it would be a wonderful thing to do. She called it a "servile work of mercy."

"You will receive graces for doing this, Henry!" Henry's mother said to him.

Henry figured he'd be blessed somehow but always wanted to see the courtyard anyway.

The convent was right next to the Cathedral of St. John the Baptist on Liberty and Abercorn. It had a high wall around it. Henry always wondered what was on the other side of the wall besides nuns.

On the day Henry went to help the good sisters, he wore his Boy Scout uniform even though he would probably get it dirty from pulling weeds and cleaning rocks.

In his paramilitary outfit and scout drill sergeant-type hat, he felt like a soldier. He would later remove his hat and shirt with its pins and badges and simply work in his green khakis and T-shirt, but he marched into the convent courtyard in his Boy Scouts of America uniform. The nuns who greeted him at the front gate and led him into the courtyard said he looked like a doughboy soldier from WWI.

"A doughboy?" Henry responded, questioning the nun's rude comment. The sisters all giggled.

About the time of the doughboy joke, Sister Mary Bride, a native Savannahian and a friend of his family, came out from the convent into the courtyard and in front of the Grotto. Sister Mary Bride was dressed in her all-white habit, getting ready to go to St. Joseph Hospital, where she worked as an RN. She told Henry to pull some of the weeds away from the Grotto, especially the enshrined statue of Our Lady of Lourdes.

"Now don't get overheated, Henry," Sister Mary Bride told him. Then she kindly brought him a large glass of sweet iced tea, which she called "sun tea," explaining that she had allowed the sun to heat it in large glass jars. She then poured the tea into a glass of ice and added a slice of lemon.

Sister Mary Bride mentioned that some ninth-grade girls from the local grammar schools might come by the Grotto while he was working but that they were there to tour the school for next year.

"They will stop by and say the Rosary in front of the Grotto with one of the novices, so please step away and let them pray. Join them in prayer if you would like," she added, "And, Henry, keep your T-shirt on while in the courtyard!"

Henry smiled, and as the kind nun walked away, she turned around and said," Henry, you don't look like a doughboy. You look like a real soldier! God bless you, and may Our Lady pray for you."

It happened to be the day Margaret Conner was on a tour with the girls from Sacred Heart School, who were hoping to attend their first year of high school at St. Vincent's Academy the following school year.

SVA was founded in 1845 by a group of Mercy sisters from Baltimore who also started St. Joseph Hospital in Savannah. The school had a colorful history going back to before the Civil War. During the Civil War, for instance, the sisters presented the Montgomery Guards, the all-Irish unit from Savannah, with a hand-sewn green-and-white flag complete with shamrocks and an Irish harp. Jefferson Davis' daughter and other daughters from the first families of Georgia had attended there because they knew they'd be in good hands with the Mercy Sisters.

Mary Flannery O'Conner, who would emerge as a favorite young southern short story writer, also attended St. Vincent's Academy. Soon, she'd be known in literary circles throughout the world. Pilgrimages of sorts would take place to her home in Milledgeville after her premature death of lupus. Miss O'Connor's short stories centered around people who experienced "redemption" or a "moment of grace" despite their flawed human nature.

Henry eventually realized that "redemption" was a very good thing and maybe the only thing that mattered.

Many girls had come of age at the all-girls school. Their alumnae formed a city-wide sorority of sorts.

Margaret and Henry attended Sacred Heart together, but Henry didn't pay much attention to her until that day. Henry would sometimes talk to her around town, like when he'd make his newspaper runs and drop a bundle of the Morning News off at the glass cashier counter at Leopold's Ice Cream Store on Gwinnett and Habersham, not far from Sacred Heart School. A few times, Margaret was there with friends having an ice cream soda, so he'd say hello. Another time, on a city bus, Margaret got up from sitting with other St. Vincent's girls and came and sat down right next to Henry. All the girls laughed, including Margaret. It must have been some kind of dare girls do.

Henry never thought much of it. For some reason, he watched Margaret walk to the Grotto with her friends when he was pulling weeds that day. She crossed herself and knelt down near the statue of St. Bernadette in front of the Grotto. St. Bernadette was the young French girl who saw the Blessed Mother and called her "The Lady." At the same time, a spring had come up from the earth, and many still go to Lourdes, France, to bathe in the water and ask for physical and spiritual healing through Mary's prayers to Jesus. Replicas of the famous Grotto were built worldwide, including the one at St. Vincent's Academy.

Henry McGee observed Margaret cross herself and say her prayers. He wondered what she had prayed.

It was then that Henry noticed her outer beauty and style and her inward beauty, which seemed to be exuding from her spirit or soul. It was what the nuns at Sacred Heart had exhorted the boys to look for in a girl. Now, he knew what the nuns were trying to teach him and his rambunctious male classmates. That's what his dad must have seen in his mother, and that's why they really love each other. *I guess it has to do with what love really is,* Henry thought that day. He'd worked with Margaret at a Catholic camp in Savannah, and later, in high school, he taught catechism to children from the country. He even danced with her a few times when her name came up at high school dances on his dance card and his name on hers. He really hadn't asked her out, though, until now.

Henry had dated a little in high school, but then came the war and his hopes for college later. He didn't spend much time or money going out on dates since he didn't have much time or money. But Henry never forgot the beautiful girl with the auburn-colored hair and the blue Irish eyes who was always smiling.

Now, he and Margaret were going on a date. And to think it all started at the Grotto at a convent! It must have been arranged by angels.

Henry had arranged for Butler to go on a double date with them, but now he needs to make sure he has asked Helen out. *Otherwise, it's me, Butler, and Margaret, and that won't work,* Henry thinks.

Henry checks with his buddy, and all is fine, and the date is on, beginning Saturday at ten, "Margaret Conner Day." *That takes care of that,* Henry thinks to himself. *But for now, it's back to the construction site to check the house's progress and put that siding on.*

Chapter 16

Grandpa

"I'm going to pay a surprise visit to Grandpa," Henry announces as the boys take a break from hammering and sawing and toting 2x4s. "Ya'll have a beer. I'll be across the road."

"Sampling gin?" Jack asks jokingly.

"Yeah, Jack, sampling gin and seeing what kind of operation he's got," Henry answers. "Y'all have a beer. I'll be back in a little while."

"Don't mind if we do," Jack responds.

Henry wipes his face and torso off with a towel and puts on his T-shirt as he starts towards the gin mill.

The road is dry and sandy, and once in a while, when a car drives by, the dust rises and falls lightly in the air but lands in the marsh before it settles anywhere near the house. These are the last of the really hot, humid days on the Island and in the Deep South. *At least ocean breezes visit here, not further inland,* Henry thinks.

Henry knocks on the old man's front door. It is an old door

weathered and stained from the salt air; a row of little square windows runs along the top of it.

"Who's there?" the old man hollers from somewhere inside the house.

"It's just Henry, Grandpa!" Henry hollers back.

"Henry who?" the old man responds.

"It's Henry, Grandpa. It's just Henry!"

The door opens with difficulty and scrapes along the old wooden floor. It is essentially one room with an attempt to divide the bedroom and the kitchen with old tables and some crude cabinet and wall-work. Some oil paintings, one of sand dunes and the ocean with seagulls flying about, and another one in watercolor of a little house by the side of the road also hang. An embroidery, which reads "Bless this house and all who enter it" is on one of the walls. There are some fossils and plenty of shark teeth and Indian arrowheads lying about, as well as what Henry guesses to be ancient Indian pottery.

Crab traps and crab buoys are scattered about. Canned goods and old bottles are everywhere. Old fishing rods are hung against the walls or stand in the corners. Even a few books and "The Book," an old leather-bound Bible, lay on a couple of tables here and there.

"Do you like my bottle collection? All dug up around here. Some from the early settlers and a lot from those Yankee soldiers who camped at the battery down the way," Grandpa says. He holds one up for Henry to observe. "I like the old Ryan bottles from the Excelsior Bottleworks in Savannah. Look at this thick glass. Them old bottles would put a few lumps on your head if thrown at you! Now, look at this one, Henry," the old man says as he holds up a clear bottle. "The real old ones have rainbows inside of them."

"Yeah, I see it, Grandpa," Henry observes.

"Happens somehow from being buried in the dirt so long,"

the old man adds. "You see, Henry, rainbows aren't always in the sky; sometimes, they come in bottles!"

The old man continues to point around at the different artifacts and treasures. "I haven't found Blackbeard's buried gold yet, and if you're wondering about your hammock, it ain't there, checked years ago. Filled the holes back up, though!" the old man laughs. "I would have bought that lot for $100, but the owner was asking too much money. I figured I could eat on that all summer," he says. "It's yours anyway."

"Twenty percent of it is mine, Grandpa. The other four own twenty percent each, too," Henry explains. "Which reminds me, would you like to purchase a share? It's for sale. Twenty dollars and a lifetime of headaches from my partners."

"No thanks. You'll learn," the old man remarks.

Henry notices the bottles of juniper berry juice near another little door, along with long, clear bottles placed under the spigot of a tub since they cannot fit under a spigot in a sink, thus the name "bathtub gin." The brew is a mixture of grain alcohol, tap water, berry juice, and other ingredients.

He asks the old man, "What's that room for?" pointing towards where the juice and clear bottles are.

"You're not working for the IRS, are ya?" the old man chuckles. "Why that's my water room or medicine cabinet, I call it!" the old man answers. "It wasn't that long ago we didn't have electricity or running water on this road. Go to bed early, get up early, the way the good Lord intended, and you don't need electricity. Was born and grew up on this island, you know. I'm used to what you boys call 'hardships.'"

Henry's glance turns to the shotgun near the old man's medicine cabinet.

"That's my 'varmint gun.' I call it, a little .410," Grandpa says. "For raccoon, squirrel, opossum, snake, and an occasional rat from the marsh."

Henry hears his friends calling for him. "Henry, Henry, we need you back!"

"Henry, Henry, we need YOUR back!" they yell again.

"Thanks for the tour, Grandpa," Henry says. "Sounds like the boys need some help."

"Say, Henry, hope you all stay around awhile. It gets a little lonely out here," he says.

"We hope to, Grandpa."

"And Henry, y'all make sure you get that siding on soon. I can smell a storm and one's a coming as sure as the Lord is!" Grandpa adds. "I remember the Hurricane of 1893. I was a little feller back then and had trouble even walking against a strong breeze, never mind the 150 miles per hour winds of that hurricane. Well, maybe 120. A storm surge of thirty feet, or maybe twenty. Anyway, that hurricane wiped out almost everything on the Island except the Old Tybee Hotel. The hotel ended up burning in '09. I remember that, too. But like I said though, I can smell a storm," Grandpa adds again. "And yes, sir, there's one a com'in' sure as Judgment Day." The old man looks towards the sky as he walks Henry out of Chateau Cobb.

Henry figures the old man says that every year hurricane season begins. There are always squalls coming off the Atlantic. Only time will tell.

It is late when Henry returns, so he and Billy began their track back to Savannah, enjoying the sunset over the marshes on the way. "When you see something like that, Henry, you know there's a God. When I was on the beach in Okinawa, I wondered whether there was a God but then I figured out it's our mistakes, not God's. We have only ourselves to blame," Billy reflects. "The nuns call it free will. You remember that, Henry?"

"Yeah, we're always blaming God, my dad says, when it's

really us... not really that complicated... I think sometimes we don't want to own up to things..." Henry responds.

"Look at that, though, Henry. God is the greatest artist!" Billy says.

"Yeah, and you and I are God's works of art, right, Billy?!" Henry says making both boys laugh.

"You know, Billy, I appreciate you saying those things. That girl you like really has you thinking straight, doesn't she?" Henry remarks as they continue west on Tybee Road across Bull River Bridge and onto Wilmington Island where the road twists and turns and is shaded with an oak canopy.

"Yes, guess the good Lord meant it to be that way... to get guys on the right path.

Love is a good thing, Henry," Billy says.

"Yeah, for us anyway. I hope for our girls, too!" Henry says before observing.

"Phil Keane could paint that sunset back there. You and I couldn't, but Phil could really paint that sunset."

"Yeah, only Phil could do it justice, Henry, only Phil..."

"I remember he once wrote a poem at BC for literature class called 'The Marshes of Chatham,' sorta like the poem we were studying at the time by Sidney Lanier, 'The Marshes of Glynn,' about the marshes down near Brunswick and Jekyll Island and such. Guys made fun of it, and Phil didn't say much, but I knew he was upset. Why do guys do that? Henry asks.

"Guess we're afraid of stuff like that. I mean, we might have to think like I did on that beach fighting the Japs. I figured out then that they were just like us; they were figuring things out, too," Billy responds. "I told the chaplain about all that stuff, and he said I was becoming a man—and a good one."

The DeSoto continues on the road back to "civilization," leaving the relaxed Island life behind.

Chapter 17

The Double Date

Henry and Jack decide to take Margaret and Helen on a double date to the beach for a picnic, a swim, and a game of half-rubber. Afterward, they want to show the girls the Lot and the house and then probably go to Harris' and eat in the kitchen.

The DeSoto is running again so Henry can pick up Margaret Conner at her house. Henry becomes nervous talking with Margaret's mother, Mrs. Conner, in the parlor of the two-story Victorian home in Baldwin Park near Atlantic Avenue, but Mrs. Conner puts him at ease. Margaret is still upstairs. Her brother, John, is also visiting the house. He went to the same high school and had been in Karl's class, so that makes for a good conversation while Henry waits for Margaret with Mrs. Conner.

John is a distinguished-looking fellow. He is tall and slender, with dark brown hair combed straight back. He wears a long-sleeve white button-down oxford shirt and pleated gray wool pants. He served as a line officer in the Merchant Marines, which were militarized with the outbreak of the war.

The Merchant Marines were still true to their British roots. Lt. John Conner has an aristocratic bearing and could have stepped off of one of Her Majesty's ships when he appeared around town in his dress uniform during the war.

Henry thought he painted a contrast to his brother, Karl, who had a ruddy complexion and always seemed to dress down, especially for a captain in the Engineering Corps of the US Army. Karl would say in a southern self-debasing way, "I'm just an old dogface..." but Henry knew Captain McGee's men loved and respected him, an exceptional response from GIs towards their officers. Henry and Margaret were deeply proud of their older brothers, who they always looked up to, especially since their service overseas and at sea.

"How's Karl, Henry?" John asks.

"He's doing very well. He's still in the hospital getting eval..." Henry catches himself. "I mean, getting a physical," he says.

"I didn't know they kept you for that," John comments.

"You're right. They usually don't, but Karl is a special case since he was wounded at the war's end, and there have been some complications." Henry starts to explain.

"I didn't know Karl was wounded."

"Yeah, a Japanese Zero shot him..." Henry says.

"A Zero, wow, that's a .50 caliber round. It must have really done some serious damage."

"Well, it just grazed him, and then he fell off his bulldozer. The Zero wrecked and exploded, and he got some serious burns and broken bones and stuff," Henry explains.

"Yeah, he must have been pretty banged up. No wonder he's back in the hospital," John answers. "That can take a while to get over. I'm sorry."

"Yeah, John, and I think the tractor turned over and exploded too and..." Henry says.

"I'm glad you told me, Henry, I may contact him..." John says.

"Oh no, he's doing better, and besides, he doesn't like anyone bringing it up. So, just light a candle for him at Sacred Heart at the Blessed Mother altar and say an Ave Maria. That's what our mother does," Henry answers. "In fact, you might want to light another one at the altar of St. Joseph...that's what my mother does too sometimes."

"That bad, huh, Henry?" John asks.

"Yeah, he's a war hero, John," Henry adds.

"I'll say," John replies.

"Enough war stories, boys," Mrs. Conner chides, then turns her attention upstairs. "Margaret, oh Margaret!"

Margaret Conner comes down the steps looking like an angel descending from heaven. Henry is overcome by her appearance and watches her every move as she descends closer to earth. She smiles with that infectious smile that lights up her youthful Irish face and makes her rosy cheeks, rosier and blue eyes, bluer, that lifts Henry's soul. She is dressed in khaki pants, tan leather-type sandals, and a white blouse with the top two buttons unfastened to reveal a small gold Miraculous Medal.

I'll have to remember to tell her I wear a Miraculous Medal, too, Henry thinks to himself.

Her auburn-colored hair is pulled back with a black plastic barrette. She carries a floral-colored beach bag. Mrs. Conner hands Henry the picnic basket sitting on the hall tree in the foyer of the stately Conner residence.

"Well, Henry and Margaret, do be careful and have fun. By the way, your mother told me at the bookstore how much you have wanted to ask Margaret out, but you were too shy to do anything. We're glad you finally did, Henry!" Mrs. Conner says.

Henry turns a little red in the face.

"Oh, Momma, stop it. Henry is his own man, aren't you, Henry?" Margaret asks.

"Well, except when my mother talks about me in the Catholic bookstore. Good day, Mrs. Conner," Henry says.

Mrs. Conner and John laugh and reply, "Good day!"

John adds, "And Henry, tell Karl I'm pulling for him."

"Oh, I will. The priest already gave him Last Rites, and he got better again," Henry remarks.

"A miracle, Henry!" Mrs. Conner adds.

"Please don't say anything about the Last Rites to my mother, Mrs. Conner. I don't want her to have a stroke," Henry adds.

"Now, here's the picnic basket with the sandwiches, and Jack and Helen are bringing the cooler with the sodas, right Margaret?" Mrs. Conner asks.

"Yes, ma'am," Margaret replies.

"And Henry is supplying the transportation, so you're all set," Mrs. Conner adds.

"And the car is in tip-top shape, Mrs. Conner. Lafayette Adams and I checked it out," Henry says.

"The Adams' boy?" Mrs. Conner asks, sounding concerned.

"Oh, mostly me, Mrs. Conner. I was just showing Lafayette how to work on cars."

"Such a caring man," Mrs Conner says to John as Henry walks Helen to his DeSoto.

"He sure worries about his family a lot," John observes, "Maybe he got wounded in the war too—in the head," John says laughing.

"Now, John, be nice. Henry was just a little nervous, and he's proud of his brother Karl, which he should be," Mrs. McGee says.

"A little nervous?" John exclaims." I think the boy's in love with my sister!"

"I don't know, but he's a good boy, and the McGees are nice people. He's already building a house at Tybee. Isn't that amazing?" Mrs. Conner comments.

Henry and Margaret laugh about Henry being interrogated by his family, then begin talking about Sacred Heart School, high school, college, and nursing school. Margaret has already graduated from nursing school and passed the state board. She is an RN working at St. Joseph Hospital, and she loves it. Henry has one more year of junior college and hopes to go to law school somewhere. They pick up Jack and Helen at the Burns' house and drive to Tybee down US 80.

Henry quietly prays that the DeSoto gets them all there and back.

Both boys begin to tell the girls about their house at the beach.

"Yes, we call ourselves the Coastal Builders," Jack tells Margaret.

"I thought you were going to school like Henry, Jack?" Margaret asks.

"I am, but we both took the summer off, and we're building at the beach. We hope to sell the property and start another house," Jack explains.

"Oh, Jack, stop. Margaret and I talk, and we know it's a place where you, my brother, Phil Keane, and that Lafayette guy can drink beer and fish," Helen says. "That's what Billy tells everyone anyway."

"Maybe it's a bit of both," Jack answers with a laugh.

The DeSoto cruises nicely down the Tybee Road. It's late in the season, but the couples still pass the peach stands, trucks selling boiled peanuts, crab salesmen, and cane pole fishers. Shrimp boats are coming in from the ocean with seagulls flying around them. A freighter appears in the distance, going out to sea from the north channel on their left.

"Daddy's ship left by the north channel," Margaret says.

"Yeah, I remember the memorial service at Sacred Heart and how you presented a sabre to the Cadet Colonel in his memory," Henry says.

"You remember all that, Henry?" Margaret asks.

"Yes, and I remember Chief Engineer Conner in his uniform. He used to stop at Segall's Store on Price and 39th Street, where I used to work after school. He bought candy for you before he went home to your house in Baldwin Park," Henry also says. "He was a real gentleman."

"Oh, he was!" Margaret says.

"Wasn't I the Cadet Colonel that year, Henry?" Jack asks.

"No, that was our sophomore year, Jack. You were only a corporal back then," Henry says.

"Henry was one of my lieutenants when I was the Cadet Colonel, girls," Jack adds.

"I bet he was your best lieutenant, Colonel," Margaret says.

Both Helen and Margaret give an overexaggerated salute that makes everyone laugh. Henry and Jack salute back in response.

"We're coming up on the construction site now, down that road to the right, ladies," Jack announces as they approach the sandy road.

"We'll show you the Lot and partially constructed house on the way out," Henry adds.

"Why didn't you build it closer to the ocean?" Helen asks.

"Oh, we like the quiet of the Back River area," Henry says.

"And we don't want a direct hit from a hurricane off the Atlantic," Jack adds.

"Unless it comes up the Back River," Margaret comments.

Chapter 18

The Sandy Shores

"We're almost to the ocean," Henry calls out as the car continues toward the beach. "The water looks great, and it's not too crowded. Let's go down near the Pavilion."

The couples change in the bathhouses near the Pavilion on 16th Street and stretch out on the beach, bringing their picnic baskets, coolers, towels, half-rubber balls, and broomsticks.

"We'll find a few others and play some away from the crowd," Jack says.

They all enjoy sandwiches, soda, and bottled beer. The girls rent an umbrella so they won't get too burned. Jack and Henry are about to finish a game of half-rubber with several other men as small waves come in one after the other. There is a strong breeze, and the gulls fly against the wind, remaining almost fixed in the air near the beach's ground.

Sandpipers, fiddlers, and ghost crabs scurry about the wet sand as the little waves come in. The ghost crabs, especially, are elusive and move quickly, walking sideways on their stilted legs back and forth between the ocean waters and their underground hiding places.

"Ever try to catch one of those things, Henry? You can't!" Jack states.

"Use to catch 'em all the time as a kid, Jack," Henry teases.

"Give you a dollar if you catch one," Jack says, provoking Henry.

Suddenly, Henry takes off after one of them. He runs, skips, turns, and twists as he chases the fast-moving and elusive "ghost crab." All, including Henry, laugh heartily. Henry ends up down near the surf without a ghost crab and dives into an incoming wave. Jack joins him. Margaret and Helen watch on as they wade along the edge. A young boy near the sea wall sells little brown bags of boiled green peanuts in a little basket he carries around. He sings to you if you pay him an extra nickel. Vendors rent umbrellas, chairs, cots, and floats. Families build sandcastles and men and women fish from the Pavilion. Another summer is coming to a close as Labor Day has passed, and it officially becomes off-season.

The two couples pack up and return to the bathhouses to change again. They take time to walk underneath the Pavilion as the tide rushes and swirls around the pilings. They climb some steps up to the veranda and onto a large dance floor, but there is no big band music and dancing that day.

Instead, vendors sell hot dogs and hamburgers, chips and Coke, snow cones, and Neapolitan ice cream sandwiches between waffle-like wafers. There is a display of oil paintings of different coastal scenes, along with someone doing charcoal sketches of faces and cutting out profiles of people on black paper.

The Southern Candy Kitchen, a popular little booth in one of the corners of the Pavilion, sells divinity, fudge, pralines, and pecan rolls that disappear quickly before they even begin to melt after being removed from a little ice box. These home-made candies were sold decades ago during Reconstruction after the Civil War and helped many southern families recover from the economic woes of the times. There is saltwater taffy "from Tybee" in colorful boxes and postcards to send to the folks back home. Other vendors have left for the season. Soon, everything will be tucked away for the fall and winter.

The girls have gone to the public restrooms again.

"Why are girls always going to the restroom together, Henry?" Jack asks.

"I don't know any better than you...I don't have sisters, either," Henry answers.

"I think guys with sisters don't know..." Jack says.

"Another mystery of life," Henry adds.

"I think they sometimes go to talk about what jerks guys can be," Jack notes.

"Probably...and we are," Henry says.

"Or they could be discussing how cute we are!" They both laugh.

"Here they come," Henry says.

"Let's go visit the Lot!" Henry announces.

"Great!" Margaret says.

"Peg O' My Heart" plays on the juke-box again. It's a big hit this summer, and the couples walk down the steps of the Pavilion, shower off the sand on their feet near the bathhouses, and start back to the car. But first, Jack runs and buys four frozen candy bars on a stick: two Zero bars and two Milky Ways.

"We get the Zeros, Jack," Henry says.

"Doesn't get any better than this, Henry," Jack says as they return to the DeSoto. The windows have been left open, but it's still hot inside. When the DeSoto starts right away, Henry sends up a silent, *Thank you, Lord.*

As they drive north on Butler Avenue, they ride by the Island Market and see Billy outside talking to a young, pretty girl with long black hair and an olive complexion.

"Pull over, Henry; let's see if he wants to ride back with us," Jack says.

Billy spots the DeSoto and says, "Y'all got to meet Lucy! Her dad manages the market, and she works here full-time. She finished Savannah High last year and knows some of the same people we do. She's really pretty and nice, too. I've asked her to 'Jake's,' but she says her father won't let her go there, so I asked her to go to dinner instead," Billy continues.

"Well, did she say yes, Billy?" Helen asks.

"Oh yes, she likes me, sis!" Billy answers.

"That's great, Billy," Henry says, "Now what about the house?"

"Oh, we're not that serious," Billy answers.

"Uh, Billy, I think Henry is asking about the house we are trying to build on the hammock at the Lot we all own," Jack reminds Billy.

"Oh, sorry, I was lost there for a second," Billy answers. "I'll be back sometime to help with... What are we doing at the house now?" he asks but immediately goes on talking. "Listen, I've got to go; Lucy needs me to help her unload the beer truck. Her dad doesn't like her lifting cases of beer," he explains. "I'll see y'all after a while," Billy says as he dashes to the back of the store.

"So long, Billy. Your sister loves you!" Helen calls out.

"Me too, sis!" Billy answers.

"And I'm in love with Lucy, the pretty little girl who works at the market, and if I, Billy Burns, ever break her heart, her daddy will have me 'kneecapped,'" Jack says, laughing.

"Oh, Jack, stop," Helen says, "I'm happy for my brother."

"Yes, Jack, that's good for Billy," Margaret states..

"And Lucy," Henry adds.

"Yes, Lucy too, Henry," Margaret says.

"Yes, Lucy, most especially!" Helen says.

———

As Jack, Henry, and the girls drive down the sandy road to the Lot, they see a pickup truck parked on the side and then Phil Keane on top of the house's roof, nailing shingles.

"He's shown up again, and he's unloaded the siding, Jack," Henry says.

"Yeah, he's come through," Jack responds.

The boys begin to make a plan for next week.

"Billy was here, and the first thing I know, he's gone. He's been going to the market down the way again. I found out he's in love with the owner's daughter," Phil says.

"We just ran into him and could see he was going in that direction," Jack responds. "Billy said he'd need a dispensation for a 'mixed marriage,' an Irishman and an Italian," Phil adds, smiling. "Needless to say, I don't think we're gonna get a lot of help from Billy."

"Yeah, and I talked with Lafayette. He wants his cut back… says we can buy him out. Nice of him, heh? He's in love, too, and won't be helping even when he gets back," Jack adds.

"Forget about all that. We only have this week to finish the house," Henry says.

"I guess I'll see you tomorrow," Jack says.

"And the next day, and the next." "I guess right now we need to get back to Savannah!" Henry says as he calls out to the girls, who are back at the car talking to Grandpa.

"Did Grandpa try to sell you any Lexor girls?" Jack asks.

"Any what?" Helen asks.

"Never mind," Jack says.

The ride back is nice, and the breeze from the side vent windows is welcoming.

They're almost back on Victory Drive when Margaret says, "I've been thinking, especially with the breeze coming in the car, do you know you boys have the roof on but not the siding?"

"So?" Jack says.

"Well, we rented an umbrella earlier, and the wind kept lifting it until you fellows put it in the ground and tilted it back. And there wasn't a lot of wind," Margaret says.

"Yeah?" Jack says.

"I think I know what Margaret is saying," Henry says. "If there is a lot of wind, your roof comes off!"

"Yes, sirree, Bob," Margaret replies.

We'll fix it tomorrow and the next day," Henry answers.

The traffic is a lot lighter than it was several weeks ago, but there's still activity on US 80 and along the side of the highway and bridges. Some fishermen are even casting for shrimp in the tidal creeks, and Henry McGee remembers being taught that by his father on the beach at Sullivan's Island, a beach near Charleston Harbor.

Sullivan's Island is to Charleston what Tybee is to Savannah. Henry identifies with both, though he has more memories of Tybee having grown up in Savannah and having just visited Charleston over the years.

"Dad showed me how to cast a net," Henry says.

"Yeah, my dad taught me too," Jack says.

"It's hard work standing on the bow of a boat and casting for shrimp as your dad guides a little bateau through the creeks hollering out orders," Jack explains. "And when I'd slip and fall, I'd have to get back up and keep casting."

"My dad used to say, 'Son, if you were an Indian, you'd be a skinny one!'" Henry says and the girls laugh.

"Hard work, but I learned to cast," Jack said.

"Glad my dad taught me on the banks!" Henry says. He had learned to throw a good cast where the whole net opened and formed a complete circular shape, opening the net. He'd practice for hours as a boy until he got it right. Once or twice, at most, he forgot to open his mouth and let go with his teeth at one end of the net, causing the net to come back on him and the weights tied to the net to hit his face.

Henry thinks he'll cast from the dock deck they'd build later to the tidal creek behind the hammock. In fact, he says he'll buy a little skiff with an outboard on it, tie it up to the dock, and name it The Margaret in honor of Margaret Conner. He knows Phil Keane would always be willing to go fish and patrol Lazaretto Creek and the little tributaries running from it.

"Heck, if I can throw it far enough, I'll cast it from the back porch!" Henry chuckles before adding, "Yes, girls, we'll have to close that umbrella tomorrow."

The DeSoto passes another marsh shack known for its seafood along the highway just as they cross the little island before the Wilmington River Bridge, which leads to Thunderbolt and home.

Chapter 19

Engaged

As planned, the four stop at Johnny Harris on Victory Drive, which is already crowded. Henry finds a parking space under a giant oak to cool off his DeSoto.

The group is waved back to the kitchen. All had covered their bathing suits with proper attire, but the big dining hall required a coat and tie.

"Oh, it's so romantic in the great room!" Helen says.

"Yes, a lighthouse, starlit ceiling, and soft music," Margaret says.

"And barbecue spare ribs," Jack adds.

The couples slip into a booth in the kitchen, a Johnny Harris tradition. They order lamb sandwiches, spare ribs, and the famous fried chicken without batter. It's all good, as always. Folks wave and greet one another. Margaret and Helen excuse themselves to go to the restroom again.

"Helen and I are serious, Henry," Jack says.

"Oh, I hadn't noticed," Henry answers.

"Henry, really?!" Jack answers back.

"I know, Jack. Helen is a fine woman," Henry says.

Helen returns to the booth, and Henry and Margaret end up in the bar talking with a group of priests from Sacred Heart and Blessed Sacrament Churches.

Henry tells the priests about their "retreat house" as Margaret stands and listens.

"Father Damien, we'd sure like it if you could stop by and bless the house if you are at Tybee," Henry says.

Margaret taps Henry on the shoulder and points over to their table. Jack is motioning them back over. "Excuse us, Reverend Fathers. We have to go now," Margaret says as she holds Henry by the hand and pulls him away from the priests' table.

When they return to the booth, Jack and Helen have already ordered dessert. They are close to each other, and Helen is holding onto Jack's arm with both hands.

"Well, are you going to congratulate us and say, 'Best Wishes'?" Jack asks Henry and Margaret.

"What?!" Henry exclaims.

"We're getting married! Jack just asked, and I said YES!" Helen exclaims, trying not to tell the whole kitchen, which is noisy anyway.

"Oh, Helen!" Margaret says as she hugs her.

"Jack?!" Henry says.

"Huh, er, hey, congratulations!" He shakes Jack's hand.

"The question just kind of popped out," Jack says. "No date yet."

"Well, Father Damien's in the bar..." Henry says as they all laugh.

"Not now, Henry, but soon," Helen says, crying while smiling and holding onto her beau.

"Still a deal?" Henry asks Jack as they let the girls in the car after paying the bill.

"Of course, Henry, nothing changes," Jack assures his friend.

"I don't know about that," Henry responds.

"I'll let you and Helen off at the Burns'?" Henry asks.

"Yeah, got to talk to Mr. Burns," Jack says.

"Good luck, Colonel," Henry says.

"Thank you, Lieutenant," Jack answers.

Henry slaps Jack on the back as he lets the newly engaged couple out of the DeSoto and into the Burns' front yard on an oversized lot near the Herb River off LaRoche Avenue. Neighborhood kids are running around and playing on a tire swing. Summer's coming to an end.

"Now Baldwin Park and then Lincoln and Maupas," Henry says as he and Margaret watch the newly engaged couple greet the kids as they walk towards the Burns' house, holding each other's hands. "Guess they better get used to greeting the kids," Henry comments.

"Oh, I hope they have lots!" Margaret says.

Henry brings Margaret to her house, and the two sit for a moment in the DeSoto, talking about Jack and Helen and how it's a good thing. "It seemed to happen so fast, but they go together," they conclude.

Then Mrs. Conner calls out Margaret's name. Margaret jumps out of the car, and Henry hurries out to open the door and walks Margaret to the front door. Margaret hugs and kisses Henry on the cheek, and Henry about passes out.

"Call me, Henry, and come by soon!" Margaret shouts as she slips inside the Conner house.

"What a day. Oh, what a day!" Henry sighs happily.

Henry parks the DeSoto and walks in the back door to the kitchen. He hears his mother and dad talking to his brother, Karl. He can hardly believe it. Karl is back home after only being home once since the war ended.

"Karl, you look great!" Henry cries out as the two men shake hands and then embrace.

"Got in earlier from Travis Field, flew in last night from Leavenworth. Passed everything and signed up again, kept my captain bars too," Karl explains.

"Gosh, it's good to have you home," Henry says, smiling.

"Just for a few days, and then I'm being shipped out to Japan!"

"Wow, speaking of Japan...?" Henry begins.

"Yes, Sue is coming with me. I'm married, brother. The base chaplain, Father Ryan, did the wedding last week. Sue is back at the base with her parents. They had all been in a relocation camp, but all that's over. Thank God they're patriotic Americans, even after all they've been through. They are devout, wonderful people," Karl says.

"Mother and Dad understand I had to tie the knot. Some of it's just the lifestyle in the military. Right, Mother?"

"Well, I'd like to have tried to go out there by train, but the main thing is it's been blessed," Mrs. McGee says.

"Yes, Mother, and besides, she's..." Karl makes the Sign of the Cross.

Mrs. McGee makes one too.

"That's great, son," Mr. McGee adds.

"Okay, now you boys go out on the porch and visit, and I'll get the dishes with Dad, right, dear?" Mrs. McGee says.

As the brothers walk to the porch with beers, Karl says, "Tina didn't seem to like it at first either. She said to me, 'Why are you marrying her?' I simply told her because I love her, Tina. And she said, 'Give God the glory, Karl, Give God the glory!'"

"I do give God the glory," Karl adds.

"Everyone is getting married, or it seems that way. Jack, Billy, and you, and I believe Laf is already married. I also heard about a bunch of others. Some in the church and some with JPs," Henry observes.

"We're making up for lost time, Henry. What about you?" Karl asks with a smile.

Henry smiled. "I have a girl, but I want to go to law school after I graduate from Armstrong College." Henry declares.

"Yeah, we'll need lawyers," Karl states.

"Post-war boom years, building and development and lawsuits." They both laugh.

"Tell me what they did to you in the psych ward?" Henry asks.

"They just ran a bunch of tests, but one day, I got impatient and left. I shouldn't have, but I wanted to see Sue. The hospital sent orderlies after me. I mean, it was just the park across the street. But the MPs came, and they escorted me back. And no, I wasn't in my hospital gown with my butt showing. I put on a sports coat and, yes, trousers, you know," Karl says. "It was a little much, but that's the Army. I thought it had to do with Sue. So, I got an Army attorney, and he helped a lot. I finished the tests, passed, and am 'certified sane by the US Government.' I kept my commission and reenlisted for as long as they'll have me. They need engineers, so I'll be staying with the engineers, going to school and building in Japan—not moving wreckage off bombed airfields," Karl explains.

"That's great, Karl. But speaking of airfields and Zeros and things, do you ever talk to John Conner?" Henry asks.

"Not since high school," Karl says. "But Mom told me you like his sister, Margaret," Karl says teasingly.

"It's more than like, Karl. She's my girl. But I was over at the Conner's house, and I got kind of nervous; you know they're kind of well off and live in a big house in Baldwin Park, and I sort of told them you were still recovering from war wounds. I don't know what overcame me. I'm just so proud of you and..." Henry nervously explains.

"Don't worry, brother. I've got you covered. If I run into him, I'll tell him, 'It's nothing,'" Karl says smiling, "and of course he'll think it's something!" The brothers laugh.

"Hey, you didn't say 'little brother.' You always say 'little brother,'" Henry notes.

"I do, but you've grown up. No, you're my brother, brother, and I love you," Karl says.

"Same," Henry says back.

"And Dad told me about the Coastal Builders," Karl adds.

"Somehow, the Coastal Builders don't seem that important," Henry reflects.

"But you got to finish what you started," Karl starts to say.

"Thanks, Dad," Henry said mockingly. "I'm getting on it tomorrow."

"But first, we'll go to Mass with Mother and Dad and then go to dinner at the cafeteria. They've been great and have been through a lot themselves," Karl says.

"You're right. I'll go later for a few hours..." Henry says.

"It's hurricane season anyway. Hope you fellows didn't put on the roof before the siding..." Karl laughs.

"Oh, no, that's common sense..." Henry says hesitantly.

Chapter 20

Mass

The McGee family arrives early at Mass and sits together as a family. Their favorite priest, Fr. Damien, is offering the Mass. Mr. McGee remarks, "Thank God, his sermons are short and to the point."

Karl slips into the confessional and is out quickly. He says his penance, kneeling as the family waits for the priest to come out of the sacristy to begin the Holy Sacrifice. Henry spots the Conners Family: Mrs. Conner; John; Margaret's older sister, Ellen; and Margaret, dressed in her nursing outfit with a dark blue cape. *I need to go to St. Joseph's this afternoon,* Henry concludes. *Maybe I can develop a severe headache. Just then, the Mass begins.*

Henry observes silently in prayerful reflection the consecration of the bread and wine into the Sacred Body and Blood of Jesus. His mother, Mary St. John, was named after a nun who had been named after St. John of the Cross. She taught him to mention his special intentions in his thoughts—especially at this time. Henry prays for his family, Margaret Conner, and his friends.

It is hard for him to see exactly when the priest calls down the Holy Ghost on the gifts since the priest faces the crucifix with the congregation and with his back to the people, but he hears the ringing of the bells for the first time and knows then. At the host and chalice's elevation, Henry is certain that Our Lord is present in the Eucharistic species. The finale, as Henry calls it, comes when the priest lifts the chalice holding the host over it on the white wooden Romanesque high altar of Sacred Heart Church and chants:

"Per ipso et cum ipso et en
Ipso est tibi Deo patri omnipotente in unitate
Spiritus Sancti omnis
Honor et Gloria...
Per omnia saecula saculorem..."

And the People of God respond, "Amen!" I believe.

Father Damien had explained to him in high school catechism that the prayer was to the Triune God who now reveals Himself to be the Father, the Son, and the Holy Ghost...

"Through Him and with Him and in Him..."

Henry prays fervently—at least at this part of the Mass. Soon, Henry and the others will approach the communion rail, which divides heaven from earth in a type of "holy of holies" coming from the Jewish roots of his faith. Henry approaches the marble altar communion rail of Sacred Heart Catholic Church and kneels. He is on the threshold of heaven. The altar boy precedes the priest and holds the paten under Henry's chin. The paten ensures the due reverence afforded as the priest takes the Sacred Host from the gold ciborium and announces, "Corpus Christi."

Henry simply responds, "Amen." He pushes back from the communion rail, noticing it wobbles somewhat from years of the same. The communion line is relatively short, and communion moves quickly. He returns to his pew in reverent silence, kneels, and prays for his mother and Father, Karl and his friends...and then Margaret. He feels a sense of peace come over him that he has never felt before. Perhaps it may just be a blessing from God as he receives the Body and Blood of his Savior in the Sacred Host and prays from the heart.

After Mass, Henry sees John Conner lighting a candle at the Blessed Mother's shrine. He apparently remembered Karl and is lighting a candle for him. John must understand, having lost his father, Chief Conner, at sea and never recovering the body. He heard Ensign John Conner had been summoned up to North Carolina to look at bodies that had washed up on shore or were recovered by the Coast Guard to see if any might be his father, the chief, but there were no matches. Mrs. Conner never went to the beach or ate Atlantic Blue crabs again, such was her sorrow and devotion. Poor Mrs. Conner, Margaret, and Ellen.

Henry sees Karl walking towards John. They both kneel and pray at one of the side altars dedicated to the Blessed Mother after lighting a small candle in a blue glass votive. *I'm sure he'll tell John,"It's nothing," about his war wounds, like he said he would.*

After the cafeteria dinner and returning home with the family, Henry McGee heads to Tybee to "finish what he started." Pulling up to the Lot, he sees Phil Keane near the pickup again. Phil has a serious look on his face as he walks up to the DeSoto.

"Someone stole our siding, Henry, it's gone. I was afraid of this," Phil expresses.

"What about Grandpa? Did he see anything?" Henry asks.

"No, he's been off on his bike, but he's madder than a wet hen about someone stealing lumber or anything on 'his road!'" Phil says. "There's so much building going on now at Tybee that we're not going to find it. We'll have to order more plywood, which will cost money, and then I'll deliver it with the big truck if I can't fit it all in the pickup."

"We don't have the money," Henry says.

"I'll get some credit because we have to get that siding on..." Phil answers.

"You're right, Phil, that's a must," Henry says.

"For now, we might as well finish the roof..." Henry says.

"The wind is picking up a little, and it's overcast; a storm is coming sure as the tide. It's just a squall off the ocean—this time," Phil says.

As the squall passes, the two men continue to work on the house.

"Plenty of servile work today," Henry acknowledges.

Henry lets Phil know that Jack is engaged. Phil mentions that Billy has been here, but he's down at the market again, helping the owner's daughter. The good news is Billy has stopped drinking and seems genuinely happy. Also, apparently, the rumors were true. Lafayette had indeed tied the knot and was very happy.

"He's always been a loyal friend, Henry, even if he's a bit of a clown at times," Phil says before starting to talk about his plans for the future.

"I'm working at the lumberyard so I can keep drawing, and I want to take courses at the local tech school so I can pursue a career in commercial art. I'd like to do beach sketching too and maybe watercolor and oils. I have sold several of these at the Pavilion; the tourists love them," Phil also says.

"You will, Phil," Henry says.

Henry glances up. "Look who is heading this way."

Billy has caught a ride and is getting out with a box of food for an early supper. The boys sit on the "beach house" flooring and enjoy sodas, ham sandwiches, and potato salad from the store deli. Billy didn't forget his friends, and they are back to enjoying their "hammock house" and talking about throwing a fishing line out into the tidal creek from their bed."

"We can enjoy the beach in the offseason and take breaks from work and study," they agree. But first, they must finish building the house.

Chapter 21

Life Lessons

It is common for returning soldiers and sailors to want to strike out on their own, get good jobs, marry, and have children. Somehow, Henry thinks that things haven't been the same since before leaving for the service. *Things will never be the same. Good, bad, or indifferent—they will never be the same.*

Henry's thoughts often drift to Margaret Conner. He imagines how it would be spending the rest of his life with someone like her, raising kids, and supporting one another "in good times and in bad, in sickness and in health." Those happy thoughts make Henry feel like he is on a perpetual natural high. He can't wait to marry and set up his and his bride's life for a future together. Margaret is beautiful, intelligent, loving, and kind. Each day, he feels them drawing closer to one another. Dare he say they're falling in love?

Margaret is deeply religious and even makes the boys she has dated wait until she's finished praying before they come to the Conner house to take her out on a date—at least, that's what one of the guys who dated Margaret said about her. When the date asked her, "What took you so long to come downstairs when I was waiting to go out with you?" Margaret supposedly answered, "I was saying my prayers!" When the boy told her to "skip her prayers," she asked him to take her home and never went out with him again.

I won't be objecting to her prayers, Henry thinks to himself. *Hopefully, there will be no other suitors for Margaret Conner anyway.*

As far as the beach house, Henry is going through the motions of finishing what he started. He had been taught these life lessons and now they've become his. There are many other ones, too.

"If you dig ditches, be the best ditch digger you can be."

"Work hard, keep your mouth shut, and expect nothing until after you are forty." "Listen and observe."

"You only have to tell the truth once."

"Say your prayers."

"And get your a— to Mass on Sundays. You owe it to the Lord."

And his mother's favorite, "You only get out of Mass what you put into it."

These are just a handful of all the lessons taught to Henry McGee by his father and mother... the same lessons taught by so many fathers and mothers of the day. The mother tempered a father's firm, guiding hands with TLC and their loving call to prayer. Things were balanced and in sync. There was order and discipline and a fear of God. Mostly, it seemed there was an authentic concern for neighbors, a deep devotion to family, and loyalty to friends.

A man would rather go hungry for a while than accept a handout unless he could provide a service for it. "Your word was your bond," and a firm handshake usually took care of things. The work ethic of the day was strong, and there was simple dignity in putting in an honest day's work no matter what you did.

Sunday was for family, and the Lord.

Henry contributed both time and money to his parish church.

Like many others, going back to the country's founding fathers, Henry thought that church communities were almost as important as family. Besides, as his father would say, "You owe it to the Lord." This devotion to faith and family held the culture together and made it strong. Neighborhoods were clean and crime-free. There was rarely a need for police intervention; the neighborhood policed itself. No one ever got away with anything because, as the nuns and your parents taught you, "God was watching and saw everything!"

God was the end-all and be-all.

Yes, Henry thinks, *I must finish what I start and maybe sell my share of the completed house to someone who is not in love.* Somehow, the thought of hanging out with his friends on the weekend no longer appeals to him that much.

Once in a while, maybe, but his heart belongs to Margaret, and she is the focus of his affection, and so would their kids be one day.

Henry is lost in thought. An Irish "therapist" might counsel, "'Snap out of it!' and get back to work!" He refocuses and totes more 2x4s.

Chapter 22

Irish Green

Henry gets up the nerve to call Margaret again. He knows she'd like to see him, but he's still shy about asking her. He calls the house and the maid answers.

Thank God, Henry thinks, not wanting it to be Margaret's mother for some dumb reason.

"The Conner residence, Lilly speaking. Who is this, please?"

"Uh, this is Henry McGee... Is Miss Margaret there, please, ma'am?" Henry politely asks.

"Mrs. Conner, it's Henry McGoo or something looking for Margaret!" the maid hollers through the house.

Gosh, lady, why don't you get a cheer horn and go out to Atlantic Park and announce it to the neighborhood? Henry thinks.

"Yes, this is Mrs. Conner. How may I help you, Mr. McGoo?" she asks.

"Er, uh, this is Henry, Mrs. Conner, Henry McGee..." Henry says.

Mrs. Conner laughs and says, "Oh, I knew it was you,

Henry. I was teasing. Let me call Margaret for you. Just one moment."

"Margaret, oh, Margaret, it's Henry McGee on the phone!" Mrs. Conner announces.

Here we go again, Henry thinks.

"Hello, Henry, I was hoping you'd call," Margaret answers.

"You were?" Henry says.

"Yes, I'd like to see you someplace today. Can you?" Margaret asks.

"Why, yes, I'd like to see you too. Where?" Henry asks.

"Meet me at the Harbor Light on Bay Street in an hour?" Margaret asks.

"I'm going now," Henry says. "Do you want me to pick you up?"

"No, John will lend me his car. See you soon, Henry," Margaret says.

"Yes, see you soon!"

Henry grabs the keys to his DeSoto and runs out of the house. He wants to get there first. It's a safe place, but sometimes there are what his mother calls "Bay Street Cadets" around. I don't want them ruining things. I'll run them off or ask some cop on the beat to do it.

Henry heads to the River and Emmett Park, where the Old Harbor Light is. It is a historical light post to greet ships coming into the Savannah Port. The light is high on the bluff at the very east end of the park. Emmett Park is a place that the Old Fort Irish from the cathedral called "The Green" or "The Irish Green." The Green was once where many people lived behind the Cathedral of St. John the Baptist north to the Savannah River. Many attended the Cathedral; later, girls attended St. Vincent's Academy, run by the Sisters of Mercy since 1845. The people were mostly of Irish parentage. They wanted to honor one of their heroes in their new home of Georgia and

America. Consequently, in 1902, Emmett Park was named for an Irish patriot who led an unsuccessful uprising in Dublin for Irish independence in the late 19th Century.

Henry McGee figures it is a good place to meet Margaret Conner but wonders what the meeting will be about. *Maybe she wants to dump me,* he thinks. "Who knows?!" he says, shaking his head.

Henry gets to Bay Street and the park in no time. The Harbor Light is not burning yet, as plenty of light still exists. He parks his DeSoto and spots a Bay Street Cadet right away, and not just any Bay Street Cadet. The old-looking man, unshaven, with an old dirty suit on and a brown fedora hat, is Willie Finn, a local WWI hero who took to the booze. Old Willie has his VA check from the government mailed to a Bay Street bar and drinks until he has nothing left. The bartender seems to be fair about his tab. When he runs out, he tries to find odd jobs like sweeping people's porches and outside their houses.

Everyone in this old neighborhood knows Willie, as he grew up here. The old residents who still know him sort of look after him. The police in the nearby Savannah Police Barracks on Habersham and Oglethorpe are patient with him, too. The firemen at Fire Station No. 1, also nearby, are friendly to him as well.

That was changing, though, as people began to move past Henry Street and even further south towards the dirt road that ran east and west across the outskirts of the city, to Derenne Road. Henry's father once brought Karl there to shoot tin cans with a .22 rifle before the war.

Henry thinks, *That's the one Bay Street Cadet I could never ignore.* Willie had been in The Meuse-Argonne Offensive on the western front in France. He had saved many lives as an infantryman under heavy artillery and intense gunfire. As a result, he was heavily decorated and hailed as a hero throughout Savannah and Georgia.

He was never the same as sometimes war veterans aren't, but a "harmless soul," as his mother would say, and a friend of his dad's. Henry's dad would even bring lunch for Willie and himself and eat with him in The Green.

"Willie, it's me, Henry McGee!" Henry calls out.

Willie looks up and seems surprised and almost embarrassed. He walks quickly across Bay Street, avoiding a meeting with Henry. *I guess he's embarrassed for me to see him or something,* Henry thinks. *He seems to be okay with Dad, though,* and Henry wonders why. Guilt and shame can be disabling, Henry guesses.

Margaret soon pulls up in her brother's car, gets out, and surprises Henry with a nice long hug. She then takes Henry by the hand and walks him to the Harbor Light.

Margaret says, "Mother, Ellen, and I used to drop Daddy off at the port west of here near the Talmadge Bridge, and then Momma would drive our car to here where we'd get out and wave to Daddy's ship as it navigated the Savannah River to the north channel and beyond Tybee. I wanted you to see the view. You are a returning sailor, and I thought you would appreciate it. Yes, Daddy knew when he saw the harbor light that he was finally safe in the harbor."

Henry struggled with his emotions and wanted to comment. Finally, he mustered up the courage. "I appreciate the view, Margaret, but..." he says, "I appreciate you a whole lot more..."

"Henry!" Margaret says.

"Er, yes, Margaret?"

"That's the nicest thing anyone has ever said to me!" she says.

Henry and Margaret talk for a long time, walking up and

down the Strand. Margaret remembered Henry having long bangs in grammar school and how he would move his head to get them out of his eyes.

"I always thought you were a smart aleck," she says.

"Smart, maybe—okay, sometimes a smart aleck," Henry responds.

The ice was broken, and Henry felt like a million, even a knight. He could talk for days, walking around the park in his new shining suit of armor.

"Oh, Henry, I've got to go. Mother will be looking for me, and John will want his car tonight. He's dating a really pretty Cajun girl from Port Wentworth who was Miss Savannah High School. I've got to go, but Helen and I will bring you all lunch the next time you're at the Lot; please call me and let me know when y'all are going," Margaret says. "I think it's a great house!"

As Henry begins to walk away, Margaret turns and calls to him from the open door, "Good night, Mr. McGoo."

Henry turns and smiles and says, "Good night, Peg O' My Heart."

I can't believe I said that! Henry smiles to himself as he begins to walk away. But something makes him stop. He turns back to find Margaret still at the car door, and she is smiling even more.

Chapter 23

Boys of Summer

The stolen lumber from their worksite seems to have affected Grandpa more than anyone. He begins asking other builders on the Island to see their plywood, not that he would recognize the stolen property. He tells them that the wood has special markings and the Tybee Police Department is working on the case. He also mentions that he sits at the window of his own shack with a double-barrel shotgun, ready to let loose on would-be thieves.

"He's really trying to help in his own way," Jack remarked.

"He's a good neighbor," Billy remarks, then adds, "I know I took 'the pledge,' but he does make good bathtub gin!"

"Yeah, maybe he's afraid the same thieves will be back and steal his gin," Jack comments.

"He keeps bringing up the hurricanes down in Florida and whether we know where they're at," Henry says.

"What hurricanes? And where?" Billy remarks.

"In South America, so don't worry about it, Billy," Jack responds.

Henry thought of the "Hurricane Lady" that he, his mom, and dad had seen in a chapel while attending Mass on a family trip to St. Augustine. As the story goes, in 1850, a Spanish ship ran into a hurricane in the Atlantic and, after discovering a statue of the Blessed Mother amongst the ship's cargo, prayed to the Blessed Mother for assistance. The ship survived the storm, and the grateful sailors gave the statue to a devout family in St. Augustine whose members were descended from the early Spanish settlers of that city. The family then gave the statue to the Sisters of St. Joseph and it came to be known as the "Hurricane Lady." People invoke the prayers of the Hurricane Lady during storms on the coast. Henry thought that if the doomsayers were right, they might need the prayers of the Hurricane Lady and Father Hurricane.

The storm from Cape Sable is moving north to the Georgia coast but hopefully will turn east towards the Atlantic. No one is quite sure where the tropical storm is now. *Has a hurricane suddenly disappeared or been lost?* they wonder.

There's nothing else the boys can do but clean up the site, batten down some of the extra lumber that wasn't stolen, and brace some of the 2x4s. They were happy to get some help from one of Jack's brothers, Pat. He is a little younger and eager to learn but asks too many questions. The boys were able to finish everything they could by Tuesday, so they took a break for the day and stopped off at Jake's for some crabs, beer, and soda for the younger Butler boy and Billy.

Jake explains, "There are no crabs; something is happening, and the crabs are out in deep water. But they'll be back, so have some hot dogs on the house. The beer you pay for and leave a tip for the help. Thanks for your service, fellows."

"Sounds great!" the boys call out.

Back at the Lot, Jack says, "Helen and Margaret are talking

about coming here tomorrow with dinner. Hopefully, Phil will get to deliver the siding. We still have time. He's having to bring the plywood to the store owners who are taking the precaution of boarding up their businesses."

Most of Savannah is built on a bluff, and when a storm hits, even at high tide, the water runs off back into the Atlantic. The barrier islands don't have that advantage as they are at sea level, nature's way of protecting the coast. The islands really weren't meant for high development, and only a few businesses and island residents traditionally live there. Things may change with the postwar boom, but for now, Tybee stays the same, relatively undeveloped and underpopulated as nature intended. Tropical depressions, spring tides that cover Tybee Road, and an occasional hurricane are all part of life at the beach.

Henry figures they only had a few more workdays at the Lot, and, if necessary, he can work weekends, as the Coastal Builders break for the year. He is slightly happy that the lumber hasn't been delivered and there is no work to do. He takes that opportunity to go home to see Karl before he leaves for Japan.

Walking in the front door, he can hear Perry Como's 'Prisoner of Love" playing on the family radio in the parlor.

Alone from night to night, you'll find me
Too weak to break the chains that bind me
I need no shackles to remind me. I'm just a pris-
　　　oner of love...

"And I'm loving every minute of it," Henry says to himself. He's never been so happy.

Life is good despite the men falling in love. They still plan to get together with the fellows. "Men's night out," it's called, and they all had agreed. But for now, Henry sits on the screened-in porch at his house on Lincoln and Maupas. It's a little cooler than usual and a little more quiet as well, almost eerily so. A red-winged blackbird swoops by in silence, lands on a small fig tree branch nearby, looks hither thither, and flies away, not making a sound. Henry thinks of what his dad says about the red-winged blackbird, "It is just a common blackbird that has discovered the color inside itself... and so must we." *Wonder what the Yuchi Indians believed the red-winged blackbird represented?* Henry asks himself.

Henry knows he and his buddies must work fast to finish the project. Chances are they won't finish since college classes are beginning. As he sits thinking about the house and Margaret, he feels a paper tucked in one of the back pockets of his jeans. He reaches for the piece of paper from his work pants and pulls it out. It is worn and difficult to read due to the perspiration and wear. "Must have forgotten I stuck it in my back pocket," Henry says to himself. It is an old receipt for lumber, but on the back is a crude but good sketch of the house at the Lot in its completed form. *Drawn from a vivid imagination, that's for sure,* Henry thinks. *It is more art than anything.*

Below the sketch is a short poem which reads:

We were the boys of summer,
Our house rises from the marsh,
She stands tall and proud, facing the squalls that
    are coming,
For how many summers?
We are the boys of seasons yet to come,
Another time is upon us.

I bet Phil Keane sketched and wrote this. Phil had discovered the color inside himself; none of the rest of us have, not yet anyway, Henry thinks.

The words are haunting as Henry again thinks how the summer has ended quickly, and for now, each will go their own way, hopefully pulling together by next summer. Henry whispers to himself, remembering Phil Keane's little poem, "Another season is here, another time is upon us."

Chapter 24

Sea Hounds

As they continue to wait on the lumber, Henry and Billy decide to make use of the time. They want to see what the Lot looks like from the little tidal creek that runs behind it. They hope to build a dock running from the back porch to the creek, making it a place where the "Gang of Four" can tie their little skiff up and go fishing and explore the marshes' intricate waterways. So, they decide to take a boat trip from the marina at Lazaretto Creek Bridge to the tributary, which runs behind the Lot.

It's easy to get lost in the creeks at high or low tide. There aren't landmarks to navigate out from the little waterways, but once the tide drops, all is left in the muck. Phil would be the one to guide them as he patrolled all the rivers and creeks during the war, but he was out delivering lumber and bargaining for siding for their house.

Billy and his pop explored many of the tidal creeks in the area when they went digging for bottles on some of the little islands. Along with bottles, Billy would find shark teeth, arrowheads, and lots of little pieces of Indian pottery. He had boxes of these relics, plenty of mini balls, some Civil War buttons from both sides, and even a belt buckle that had partially disintegrated and had a partial "U" and "S" of the "US." Billy claimed the belt buckle was damaged because it was hit by a Confederate "mini ball" fired from a nearby battery and saved the Union soldier's life. Billy kept it as sort of a good luck charm.

Billy and Henry borrow a boat from Captain Sancken, a local charter boat captain who is friendly with Billy's dad. The little skiff has a two-stroke motor that makes a "ta-ta" sound. In fact, some of these boats, which fish the local waterways, are called Ta Ta's because of the sound the two-stroke outboard makes. Still, all that matters is that it gets them from point A to point B. Of course, if they break down, there is no place to thumb a ride. They would simply have to wait for a passing vessel as they are eaten up by sand gnats. Many crabbers, fishermen, and oystermen also work the waterways in this area. Some pleasure crafts but primarily working fishermen.

The cooler months of the oyster season are coming, and places like the Pin Point Community and other oyster processing plants continue to send their little wooden boats out to harvest the coveted shellfish. Pin Point, in particular, is known for its fine oysters and, in fact, packages them with a clear top to show off the quality of their product.

Henry always thought that the Pin Pointers had a culture that must have rivaled the coastal Indians. The folks out there knew how to do everything and survive off the land and river. They grew their own crops on little farms, turning dirt with the help of a mule, hunted their own wild game, fished for their own seafood, raised their own chickens and pigs, milked their own cows and goats, fixed their own vehicles, and built their own homes. An independent and self-sufficient community that boasted. "The river supplies us with all we need." The Pin Point folks called Savannah people Mainlanders. They realized people who weren't in or near the water daily didn't have a clue about what they did. Working in the oyster plant or on the river was hard, but the Pin Point natives had a pride and dignity that others recognized and respected. Their strong faith in the afterlife often kept them optimistic, hopeful, and standing tall—always moving forward. Their work ethic was second to none. Their family and faith, along with the river, were everything.

Billy is particularly excited to show Henry the secrets of the marsh. "Henry, you will remember this day as a revelation," Billy quips. Henry wonders what Billy means by a "revelation" but has learned to accept Billy's ways.

"Well, I just hope we get to see the Lot from the creek. That will be revelation enough!" Henry retorts.

The two make the now familiar trip down Victory Drive, across Wilmington Island and Whitemarsh Island, across the sacred marshland, to the bridge...Across the bridge is "Tybeeland" and the little fishing camp near the docks where the shrimp boats are moored. The bridge is up, letting some shrimp boats back into the Lazaretto Creek from the Atlantic.

"Not many gulls are circling the boats, Billy," Henry comments. "They must not have caught much."

"Either that or they know something we don't," Billy adds. "But it takes more than a squall or even a hurricane and tidal wave to give me the heebie-jeebies," Billy says. "I've faced worse, a lot worse."

"I know you have, buddy. Let's move out," Henry commands. The boats pass, and the draw part of the Bridge closes. Henry thinks of Phil's impromptu poem, *Another season is upon us,* and wonders.

They are greeted by Captain Sancken, a well-tanned, older gentleman sporting a blue Captain's cap and dressed in a long-sleeved light blue cotton seaman's shirt, khakis, and brown deck shoes.

"Howdy, boys! You must be the sea hounds!" Captain Sancken hollers.

"The sea hounds; I like that title, but we're sort of amateur sailors," Henry says.

"Speak for yourself, Henry. I practically grew up in the marsh!" Billy says.

"A marsh baby, heh, young man? You must be Mr. Burns' son, heh?"

"That's right, Burns is my name, Billy Burns. Mr. Burns is my pop!" Billy responds proudly.

"Come this way, sea hounds," Captain Sancken commands as he leads the two boys to the docks.

"Yes, sir!" the boys answer.

"Here she is, your own skiff with a two-stroke outboard, filled up and ready for the 'low seas!'" the captain says, laughing. Pointing to the inside of the boat, the captain says, "There are the oars in case the motor gives out, but it should be okay. Hope you know the waterways. Easy to get caught up in those little creeks. Tide is coming in, though. You should be okay for the day." The captain waves and walks away smiling. "Bon Voyage, sea hounds!"

"Now step towards the boat's center, Billy, and let's cast off," Henry commands.

"Er, Henry, I kind of was hoping I'd be the captain of this vessel," Billy says, somewhat disappointed.

"Oh, that's fine, Billy. You can be the captain, and I'll be the first mate," Henry responds.

"Great! Now step towards the center, Henry, and cast off!" Billy orders. The two push away from the dock, and the outboard starts without a problem. The boys head up Lazaretto Creek and into the marshes of Chatham.

"Billy, look over there; the dolphins are beaching themselves on the muddy banks!" Henry exclaims as he sees a group of dolphins pushing themselves out of the water in a wave as they rush ashore.

"No, Henry, they're fishing. Cut the motor. Let's watch for a while. My dad told me the dolphins do that on 'porpoise.' Haha, I mean 'purpose.' Working together, they trap the fish and create a wave pushing the fish up onto the banks depending on the tide. The dolphins then enjoy a buffet of whiting, speckled sea trout, and saltwater crappie," Billy proudly explains. "Watch them. They always end up on their right side to ensure the fish don't get away. The dolphins then go back into the creek and do it again and again. They have to be careful not to push themselves too far, or they'll get stranded."

"Amazing," Henry responds.

"Yeah, my dad says Savannah is the only place in the world where dolphins do this. Dad and I watch them a lot when we're exploring the marsh creeks. We have some smart dolphins around here," Billy concludes.

"I guess, but if their timing is off..." Henry observes.

"They're risk takers, like us."

"Never thought of myself as a risk taker, but with the house and all, I guess we are," Henry responds as he thinks how Billy really is a seahound or a marsh creek captain. The Boys of Summer continue their voyage with Billy as the skipper. "Where now, Billy?" Henry asks.

"I think to your left, or your port, I mean. There is an outlet that is the one we're looking for," Billy says, hesitating.

"Okay, let's turn or steer there. Now, since you're the skipper, you take the handle to the motor, and I'll use the oars to keep it from running aground. I've at least done that before," Henry says.

The sea hounds navigate their way into the tidal creek. The waterway narrows, and though the tide is coming in, the boys see nothing but marsh grass. A dolphin suddenly appears out of the water, startling the explorers but then reassuring them that the water is deepening with the incoming tide. Marsh birds fly about, and some sea otters fish in the distance. Diamondback terrapins sun themselves on the banks of the creek.

"You sure this is the creek, Skipper?" Henry asks.

"It looks like it, but then again, they all look like it," Billy says.

"Skipper?!" Henry responds.

"Calm, Sailor, it's too early to panic; we'll be fine," Billy responds.

The waterway continues to narrow, and the dolphins have disappeared.

"Maybe they were warning us, Billy. Dolphins are mammals and highly intelligent. Sometimes they even rescue humans at sea," Henry observes. "And in these parts, the dolphins even know how to go up on shore and catch fish. Tybee has some very smart dolphins."

"Henry, you're overreacting again. We are not lost, and we are not at sea. We are 'at marsh' or something," Billy says.

The waterway gets narrower and narrower and then stops, and there is nothing but a very high "wall" of marsh mud, oyster beds, and marsh grass. Billy cuts the motor. Henry pushes the boat away from the marsh grass with a single oar. There is complete silence except for a few little fish splashing and marshbird sounds.

"We have navigated to the source of this little tributary, and it is here," Henry says discouragingly.

Billy remains silent.

"I wonder if Blackbeard got lost in these little creeks too when he'd come ashore in his launches to hide his gold?" Henry asks.

"Listen, Henry, I'm a Marine, not a sailor, and I was relying on my first mate to assist me with his seamanship." Billy changes the course of his remarks and continues, "Okay, Henry, we went down the wrong 'crick.' Let's turn this Ta Ta around, go back against the tide, and go down the right one!" Billy commands. "And yes, I'm sure Blackbeard and his pirates got lost in these dagum creeks, too! And Ponce de Leon and his conquistadors, and Oglethorpe and his Redcoats... What difference does it make? Now. turnabout!" Captain Billy orders.

"Yessir!" Henry shouts.

"Bet the Yuchi Indians never got lost," Henry whispers softly under the sound of the motor. "Or Ponce de Leon. Or the Redcoats." Henry doesn't want to antagonize his good friend and the Marsh Creek skipper any further. The outboard works hard against the tide, and the boys get back to the main creek and try the next visible inlet. It seems to go somewhere, and the next thing you know, they spy the roof of the unfinished house. As the creek continues to rise, they see most of the structure from the waterway.

"There she is, Henry, our house and the Lot," Billy says excitedly.

"Land ahead!" Henry sings out. "Stop the motor, and let's drift a moment. I'll use the oars."

"I'm glad you didn't mutiny, Henry. I told you I was raised in this marsh, but it plays tricks on you like the forest," Billy remarks. "We recovered and accomplished our mission."

"A beautiful sight, Billy, a custom-built home rising out of the marsh and claiming its place in Tybee history," Henry observes.

"Yeah, I doubt that it's the finest house on the Island, but it's got character. Doesn't it?" Billy asks. "Sure does. It's got character and dignity, just no siding," Henry admits. "Phil will come through; he always does." Just then, a great blue heron lands on top of the house's roof and stands tall and proud, surveying the marshland. "Billy, look, a blue heron..." Henry whispers.

"Yeah, yeah, I see it, Henry," Billy whispers back. "What would the Yuchi Indians say it represents, Henry?"

"I think an inner peace, Billy," Henry whispers. "Something like what Phil has, and you are finding, and we all want."

"Well then, that's a good sign," Billy answers. "Let's get back to port, and if that old salt asks, 'How'd it go?' You are to respond..."

"A perfect voyage, thanks to Captain Burns!" Henry finishes. "And a revelation. Truly a revelation, Billy," Henry adds as the Boys of Summer putter back to their port of call through the little creek.

Chapter 25

Not Dorothy

Henry was pleased by the outcome of the boat excursion. He couldn't believe how lucky he and his friends were, to be building a house right on the water. But as soon as he stepped out of the boat, he began to worry about its completion. "We gotta get back to the Lot, Billy," he said.

Henry and Billy jumped in the DeSoto and began the drive to the Lot. As they crossed over Lazaretto Creek, they noticed lightning in the distance.

"Damn. You see that, Henry? It's lightning, all right, but it's different. It looks round or something," Billy said excitedly.

"It's called ball lightning," Henry says. "I've never seen it before, but I've read about it."

"Feels like another revelation, but this one isn't a good sign. Maybe the Four Horsemen of the Apocalypse," Billy notes.

"You mean the four horsemen?" Henry asks.

"Yeah, Death, Destruction, Pestilence, and Famine," Billy answers.

Henry replies, "I know the four horsemen: Stuhldreher, Miller, Crowley, Layden,..."

"No, no, Henry!" Billy exclaims, "Not the four horsemen of Notre Dame, the four horsemen in the Bible!"

"I don't read the Bible much, Billy," Henry responds.

"That's what I'm telling you, Henry. It's a warning from the heavens, right out of the Bible. Let's get to the Lot—and fast," Billy concludes.

The Savannah boys are all at the Lot when Henry and Billy arrive. Phil is supposed to make another delivery with the precious cargo of plywood for siding. All of Pat Butler's questions about the Cape Sable storm ended up helping. Henry looked into the location and strength of the tropical storm, heading for southeast Georgia from Florida and reaching parts of the coastal area further south of here when last reported. The boys didn't have much experience with hurricanes, just what they had read and seen in movies. Savannah doesn't get many direct hits, the last being over fifty years ago, but there is always fallout from the storms that pass by or hit further south in Florida.

The boys are waiting, armed with hammers, 8-penny nails, and sharpened saws. Even Grandpa is acting as a lookout for Phil's lumber truck. Jack Butler has even devised his own "batten down belts" in case the siding isn't up on time. This meeting of the brains and brawn is the grand finale of the summer of 1947.

"Maybe I'll move here and do construction," Billy says. "Lucy can help her dad at the store, and I'll tote 2x4s and say I've worked with the Coastal Builders."

"Yeah, and builders on the Island will say, 'Who the Hades are the Coastal Builders?" Jack jokes.

"The wind is really picking up, fellas. That storm must be closer than we thought and moving faster," Henry says.

"Where was it last?" Jack asks.

"Near the coastal islands south of here but off in the Atlantic. It looked like it was going out to sea, then it got lost. How does a hurricane get lost?" Henry asks.

"It doesn't, but the forecasters do," Jack explains.

"Here she blows, boys!" Grandpa hollers from up the sandy road.

The wind has really picked up, with gusts almost knocking Jack off the roof as he checks the shingles. Then the rain begins.

"It's Keane in the big truck!" Jack yells from the rooftop.

"Yes, there she blows, the lumber truck!" Billy yells, too.

The boys run out to meet Phil, who is driving in a heavy yellow colored raincoat and hat like a fisherman might wear on the truck seat.

"Do we have time?" Henry asks.

"I don't know," Phil answers slowly, looking up at the tree-tops and sky.

"Let's unload and nail up the plywood siding. The framing is ready for it, and then let's get out of here," Jack remarks.

Phil says, "I made all the other deliveries. Folks are worried; they haven't had a real hurricane in a while," Phil says as he and the others start unloading the plywood. "And the Coastal Defense Force has arrived, boys!" Phil yells.

"Do we have time?" Billy yells over the wind.

"No, it's a lost cause, just like Fort Pulaski being shelled from Tybee batteries..." Phil exclaims.

"Hate to say it, but we should surrender. Abandon ship—or house!" Phil says again.

"What about the siding?" Billy yells as the wind noise increases.

"Forget it!" Henry yells.

"Shouldn't we try?" Billy asks.

"It's too late. The velocity isn't letting down; it's increasing!" Jack calls out.

As the boys work quickly, another car appears coming down the sand road. "I don't believe it! It's Helen and Margaret in her brother's car. Good God!" Jack cries.

"What? I told her to please not try to come down here," Henry adds.

"Where was all this help last week? Now all we need is Lafayette, his bride, and Lucy to show up, and it will be complete!" Jack says.

"Next thing you know, the padre's going to show up for the blessing," Billy adds.

"Or the burial at sea," Henry says.

"Hello, boys. We have dinner just like we said," Helen calls out as they begin to unload the wicker picnic basket filled with food and the cooler with sodas. We can sit in the car and eat while we look out at the marsh and the house."

"Does the house have a name yet, Henry?" Margaret yells into the wind. "Beach houses always have names, just like ships."

"Yeah, the name will be the SS Dorothy in the *Wizard of Oz* if we don't get this siding on. The wind will definitely lift it," Henry yells. "No time for dinner, ladies," he adds. "I warned you about coming, Margaret. This storm is crazy."

Just then, a wind gust hits the group. The doors on the cars slam, causing the girls to drop the covered dishes they were unloading from the car.

"I think that hurricane may be closer than we thought," Phil says. "Must be the early gusts from what's off the coast. We need to get outta here."

"Grandpa, you got to come with us in the DeSoto. Girls, you need to turn around and return to Savannah, lickity-split," Jack says.

Henry looks around for Billy and realizes he has gone on the hammock to pick up the tools. The water has risen and the wind has increased immensely. "Now Billy's really marooned," Henry yells to the group.

"Get Billy, Henry, I'll take care of the girls!" Jack commands.

"I'll get him, Henry," Phil says as he ties a rope he brought with him to his waist and tells the others to hold it just in case they get stuck in the marsh mud. Phil jumps into the marsh. The water is so high that only the top of the grass can be seen. He also ties Billy around, and they return to the sandy road, both winded and caked with Marsh mud, coughing up seawater. The DeSoto is now half-filled with water. The girls have turned John Conner's car around and are waiting on the east side of the road as water pours onto it. Phil turns the big high truck and finally points it towards US 80.

Before jumping on the truck, Billy and Henry pause and glance back, however briefly, at the house on the hammock. They had worked so hard, trying to finish. Now, they wonder if the house will withstand the storm at all.

"We still have to name it, Billy," Henry comments.

"Helen, Margaret, or Lucy," Billy responds. "Anything, but NOT The Dorothy," Billy adds.

Chapter 26

The Hurricane Lady

"Jack, you jump in and drive the girls' car, and we will follow. Go to Jake's first and see what's going on there, then if you have to, go to Battery B at Fort Screven. Remember, you take a left at the old guardhouse to get to Battery B. It's the one you, me, and Billy explored a few weeks ago," Phil commands as he takes charge.

"Grandpa, get into the truck. Henry or Billy, one of you get in the bed. Now go!" Phil cries out.

All do as the Coast Guard Auxiliary commands. The wind gusts are increasing, and water from the marsh is surging. The rain is now almost blinding. "Throw the siding over, Henry!" Phil yells.

Henry cringes. All that siding thrown away. "This is going to hurt our wallets."

"But it will crush you if you don't!" Phil explains.

"Aye, aye, Captain!" Henry calls back.

Just then, Grandpa comes shuffling out with a couple of bottles of bathtub gin. "Sorry boys, had to fill a few up for medicinal purposes. This storm is going to cover the Island!"

Grandpa hollers. "But I got Grandpa's Lexor! Yee-ha, let's move out! Ya know, it's gotta happen once every forty years or so. It's very biblical. The last one was back in..." Grandpa starts to mumble out a hurricane history lesson.

"Quiet, Grandpa; let's move out! You can tell us later!" Phil exhorts.

"Wait! I gotta get my cat, Figaro," Grandpa exclaims. "Here, Figaro, Figaro, Figaro," he sings.

"Figaro will be fine, Grandpa. Let's go!" Phil shouts again. Phil maneuvers the truck and heads down the sandy road toward US 80. Jack and the girls are long gone; hopefully, they made it to Jake's or the battery in her brother's Plymouth. The DeSoto is lost and disappearing into the rising waters. Henry has parked it too close to the marsh.

Several people are on the road, and Phil picks them up, ordering Henry to hold them tight in the small truck bed lest they are blown off. The truck creeps across the highway past Jake's. Phil blows the horn, but no one comes out from the juke joint. He moves along slowly, stopping for several more people, including a Tybee Island police officer whose patrol car is stalled.

The officer hops on the bed and explains that the storm went out to sea and picked up strength to come barreling into Tybee. "We were caught unaware. We dropped the ball on this one. The Strand is flooded badly, and the Back River is too. The water is rising on the far north end of the Island, and parts are completely underwater," the officer explains. "Fort Screven is holding its own. The lighthouse is working like it has for over 150 years," the policeman says. "The storm will eventually plow through Savannah and all of Chatham County."

Phil stops again for a mother with two screaming children. Billy gets out, grabs all three, and puts them in the truck's cab.

Billy jumps onto the bed, and the others hold onto him and help to pull him up.

"I'm almost to the Battery," Captain Phil yells. "I'll let y'all get out. Lock arms, and watch the flying debris." Phil gets as close to the Battery's entrance as possible. Water is inside, but steps lead to a dry upper level. The group of refugees does as Phil orders, and Phil heads out for more people stranded. The police officer organizes the people inside the bunker, and Phil is gone.

Henry starts to run out, but Jack appears from inside the bunker, grabs him, and pulls him back. They both fall down from the wind gusts outside of the bunker. Helen and Margaret scream. The Tybee policeman pulls them in. He is a big man with giant arms and brute strength.

"Phil's truck is going to flip," Henry says.

"It's a heavy-duty lumber truck, son. He'll be okay as long as he doesn't run into the surge that's coming," the policeman comments. "He's a brave young man."

"Damn right," Henry says.

Meanwhile, Phil frantically looks for more stranded islanders but realizes he can't see a thing. The windows are fogged, and the rain comes pouring in as he tries to look out an open window to regain his direction. He rolls the window up again. He knows he's somewhere on the far north end. He realizes he has to find a shelter. Phil looks for stranded Tybee residents. He says an Ave Maria out loud as he was taught by his mother and the nuns.

"Hail Mary, full of grace, the Lord is with thee. Blessed art thou among women, and blessed is the fruit of thy womb..."

He sees no more stranded people; they've all found some kind of refuge, he hopes. He does not know that he's close to the worst flooding on the Island. Although high off the ground, the one-ton Ford flatbed truck is stalling due to the water and is struggling to move in any direction as the wind seems to almost flip it.

Won't be opening these doors, won't be able to close them, Phil thinks to himself. "I'm dead in the water," he mumbles to himself. "It was a dumb move coming this way, but I meant well," he prayerfully mutters to himself. "Sorry about the fool-hardiness. Guess I'm trying to make up for something," he adds. "Jesus, Mercy," he prays.

The water continues to rise and pushes hard against the truck. Phil Keane has unwittingly driven too close to the water and mouth of the Lazaretto Creek, which flows into the Savannah River channels along with the Wilmington River. The tide has also ebbed and is rushing out. The truck moves left and then right and turns all the way around. Phil tries to turn the steering wheel to no avail. The cab begins to take on water, and Phil cannot open the door due to the force. He instead rolls down the window yet again. He sees the water almost even with the door of the cab, and the force continues to push the truck further away from what he perceives to be roadway and land. Phil begins to feel the vehicle float, and it seems to bob up and down now, and more water pours into the cab.

The surge of water hits the truck, and it begins to actually float. Phil tries to gain control of the vehicle, but it is like a rudderless vessel on the high seas. Captain Phil looks up and sees the glow of the Tybee Lighthouse and again prays, this time for "those who go down to the sea."

He sees little but the truck's headliner, grey water, and pouring rain. He feels cold but doesn't panic. Instead, he continues to say some prayers and, oddly enough, begins to mention the names of family members and friends like Henry, Jack, Billy, Lafayette, Helen, and Margaret. He prays for his mom and dad, brothers and sisters, old man Cobb, Jake, and others who come to mind.

Then Phil prays for his enemies, the Germans and Japanese soldiers and sailors, and then returns to his family and friends and the Poor Souls in Purgatory. He and his truck are almost filled with water. The surge carries them further away from the dunes, towards Lazaretto Creek and the channel. Phil Keane finds himself floundering about inside the truck's cab. He rolls down his window and sticks his head outside; rain droplets hit his face as the saltwater overtakes his cab.

Phil begins to swallow water and tries to breathe. The rain is cold but refreshing as it washes the salt water from his face. He sees the raindrops hitting the surface of the storm surge. Phil attempts to swim through the window but can't until the truck turns again, and he seems to slip out with the current. He thinks he sees the light from the Tybee Lighthouse. Phil is disoriented and swims in different directions. He is weak and flounders about moving his arms back and forth and up and down. He begins to panic. An intense fear sets in.

He cries out in prayer, "My Jesus, Mercy!" then a strange euphoria comes over him, and he is suddenly free of all fear, anxiety, and worry. A woman clothed in white and in a bath of bright light seems to reach out and draw him closer. "Is this the Hurricane Lady Henry told me about?"

He seems to now rest in the bosom of the Lady who assists him in rising out of the gray waters and guides him towards a white dawn. He is suddenly awash in an intense peace that flows all about him. Phil Keane rests in glory.

Chapter 27

The Rainbow

The folks inside one of the abandoned rooms of the Battery sit and wait for the winds and the rains of the hurricane to subside and eventually pass. The temperature has dropped and there is a coolness in the damp room, which keeps them safe from the rising water and strong wind gusts.

The noise from the wind is constant, and occasionally, one could hear a power line pop and make an electrical buzzing, exploding sound. Metal objects hitting things and rolling on the paved roads can also be heard.

People in the Battery sit, some more relaxed than others. The young mother and three children, who Phil picked up in the lumber truck, hold each other, shivering from the cold rain. The mother prays for the Lord "to protect that young man who brought us here." A middle-aged man in black slacks quietly sits and smokes a cigarette, staring outside at the continued rain, which disallows any real view of what's happening. They only hear the sounds.

Grandpa is wearing an old grey raincoat, which he grabbed while he was getting his bottle of gin. He is unshaven and has a few days of beard growth. He also wears an old gray rain hat. He looks like what the old Tybee Lighthouse keeper might have looked like. He takes a drink from his gin bottle and says, as an older woman looks scornfully at him, "Berry juice for my innards." The woman turns her head disapprovingly.

He kindly offers the mother with the three children his raincoat to cover themselves. She politely refuses. Henry recognizes one of the waiters from Jake's and asks him whether Jake stayed at Jake's. The young man says he thought he was upstairs in the cinder block building with his wife, other family members, and a few friends from the Island. It's a good building, not as strong as the Battery, but solid.

"I'll see him down the road, I'm sure," Henry says, "but I think Jake's is closed for the season,"

"Yeah, we'll have a lot of cleaning up to do on the Island, but we'll be in good shape for next season," the juke joint worker says.

The policeman remains standing looking outside in his wet, blue policeman's uniform. The blue knight is vigilant. He still wears his 8-point policeman's cap and holds a flashlight in his hands, wondering if there's anything he can do further. "I hope that young man parked that truck and found shelter," the veteran policeman says aloud. "That north side down near the water is where he was heading. It floods bad and the tide is turning and moving east out to the ocean. It's moving fast."

Henry looks around again and goes and sits with Jack, Helen and Margaret.

Margaret says, "I guess I borrowed John's car once too often."

"Not your fault, Margaret. No one seems to have known how close the storm was," Henry reassures her. "But make sure you tell him that Jack and I didn't want to put you and Helen in danger."

"Mother, John, and Ellen will be worried to death," Margaret comments.

"As you are about them, Margaret. We'll contact them as soon as we can," Henry says.

The wind and the rain seem to slow, and some mistakenly think it's the eye of the storm, but it's moving further inland. The small group inside the bunker sits patiently and quietly, knowing that there is nothing they can do; it's nature's call. The hurricane continues to bear down on the little island and races towards Savannah and beyond.

The folks inside the abandoned rooms of the Battery sit and wait for the winds and rains of the hurricane to subside and eventually pass.

The small crowd of people who had sought refuge in the Battery along the north end of the Island at Fort Screven emerges from the makeshift shelter into clear skies and a resurrected sun that already seems to be soaking up the flood waters from the ocean, marshes, little creeks, and tributaries.

"Everyone okay?" the policeman hollers in a deep, loud voice.

"All good," a few respond.

Jack, Henry, Helen, Margaret, and Billy all stand together surveying the area.

"Where's Grandpa?" Billy asks.

Just then, Grandpa comes out of the Battery, calling out, "Here I am, saved by the Lexor!" Grandpa raises a bottle of his bathtub gin.

"Think some salt water got in that tub, though," Grandpa remarks. A few laugh.

"Say, look, Henry, a rainbow! That doesn't happen too often after a hurricane!" Grandpa wisely observes. "The Good Book says that the rainbow is a promise that we won't ever get completely flooded out again. It gives us hope."

"Amen," a few pray.

The water has ebbed and is rapidly running out to sea as the tide works in everyone's favor. Savannah is spared heavy damage, and true to form, the water runs off of the bluff. "The early English settlers had a good eye for real estate," people say. The barrier islands serve nature's purpose and act as a buffer, though Tybee, Jekyll Island, St. Simon's Island, and other barrier islands along the Georgia coast sustain the most damage. The sea wall built by the CPW back in the Depression holds. The jetties do their job of preventing massive erosion. There is some flooding in the businesses on 16th Street, such as Christy's Department Store and the T.S. Chu Co Building, as well as a few bars and small confectionaries.

The Carbo Hotel, a two-story wooden structure with a partial wraparound porch on both floors, fairs well. The Wilson Hotel, also on 16th Street, gets by unscathed.

Signs have fallen off the front of some of the businesses, but the familiar letters on top of T.S. Chu's entrance are intact. Even "Grandma," the Fortune Teller Lady in the little glass booth, is back reading fortunes. "Just deposit the coin in the slot, and Granny will warn you and gladden you of future events!" One gentleman later claimed he read his fortune from the Lady, and she warned him of an impending storm. He consequently ended his summer vacation and left the Island early, crediting the Fortune Teller Lady.

And right now, the future for Tybrisa is looking pretty bright. The Tybrisa Pavilion sustained some damage but held up against the waves, wind, and storm surge. The bells of St. Michael's continue to ring for prayers and beckons for Sunday Mass and services to give thanks to God the Creator.

The staff of the Fresh Air Home including Franciscan nuns

in their white habits, joins the good church people of the Island and serves hot coffee, doughnuts, and orange juice to the public.

Other bells in front of little cottages and classic Tybee homes ring, not for dinner or storm warnings, but for thanksgiving.

Of course, trees, marsh grass, debris, and even some wooden recreation and fishing boats lay on their sides or upside down near the beach. Parts of the north end and back river area have been hit with the heaviest flooding. Cars have been flooded and moved some. Rumors of caskets popping out of the little cemetery behind Tybee City Hall are untrue. There just happened to be a few crates that blew and washed up near the old graveyard and landed amongst the markers, being mistaken for wooden coffins coming up from the sandy soil. There are several dozen missing people from the Island, and all but one are eventually accounted for—in time.

The heavy-duty lumber truck Phil Keane was driving was found on a sand bar near the mouth of Lazaretto Creek. Phil is missing and remains so. His body is presumed to have washed out into the channel and ocean.

The hammock and the Lot survive the storm as they have for centuries, but the house is destroyed. All that remains is simply a pile of lumber scattered about. "Lifted up like an umbrella because there was no siding on it," as property surveyors for the county and insurance companies report. Margaret Conner could have told them that. Only pilings driven deep into the ground by the boys remain like the old pilings from the railroad, standing there with nothing to hold up anymore.

The pilings would remain for years and years, reminders of the Boys of the Summer of 1947 when they were lean and robust, returning from war and service. The pilings were also like a memorial of sorts to their buddy, Phil Keane, who always came through and was hailed as a local hero. The Savannah Morning News and Press reported that Phil Keane represented youth and energy, loyalty, and friendship. The Boys of Summer knew that to be true. A marker honoring him stands near Fort Screven and the Tybee Lighthouse, erected by his friends and the military.

"No greater love has one than to lay down his life for his friends," John 15:13.

Father Damien offers a special requiem Mass for Phil several days later at his home parish, Sacred Heart Catholic Church on Bull Street, where Phil was baptized and attended high school.

During the sermon, the priest talks about death and resurrection and Phil laying his life down for his friends. He mentions that Phil, the aspiring commercial artist, painted scenes from Tybee and the surrounding marshes, waterways, and ocean, too. The priest preaches with conviction, reminding those attending, "All things are passing. We are simply traveling. What matters is not money and fame but faith and the good works that accompany us. These are the only things that last unto eternity."

Henry McGee hangs his head as he listens to the heartfelt sermon.

Jack, Henry, Billy, and Lafayette, along with so many other family members, friends, schoolmates, and members of the community, other ministers and pastors from churches, and the rabbi from Mickve Israel Synagogue, attend the Mass and learn to let go of a real hero and entrust him to the grace and power of God. They are humble people of the day and know that their strength lies not in themselves but in the God of their fathers, the God of Abraham, Isaac, and Jacob.

Standing outside the church after Mass, the group decides to abandon the project at the Lot and go on with work, school, and their own families, which they hope to start soon. Their lives are just beginning. There will be other storms, natural and otherwise, in their lives. But they'll never forget that summer. It may have only been one chapter in their lives, but it was a very good one filled with fun, sunshine, happy times, and friends they have cherished more than ever since returning home from the war effort. They will continue to pursue their dreams and live their lives, always enjoying the simple things and having a good day at the beach.

Chapter 28

The Bridge to Everywhere

"Dad? Dad? You ready yet?" Phil asks.

Henry turns to his son, "Make sure you have a Mass said for..."

"Phil Keane," his son says, finishing Henry's sentence.

"Yes, Captain Phil Keane," the old man remarks. "And Jack Butler, Billy Burns, Lafayette Adams, and your Uncle Karl, too."

"Dad, Uncle Karl's son probably remembers his father at every Mass he offers," Phil says.

"Tell your cousin, Father Damien McGee, to remember Aunt Peg, my brother Karl, and the Boys of the Summer of 1947. He'll understand," Henry McGee instructs.

"Sure," Phil says. "What are you thinking now, Dad?"

"I'm thinking how this house was never blessed," the old man says.

"What house, Dad?" Phil asks.

"The one sitting right over there on that little hammock," the old man says.

"No house there, Dad, just a few trees and bushes. No house," Phil says softly.

"Yes, there is, son. Yes, there is. I can see it as plain as the hand before me, and I still have good eyes. In fact, I can see through that house to the creeks and marsh beyond because we put the roof on but never put the siding up, and the wind came through and lifted the house up like an umbrella, just what your mother said would happen," the old man explains.

Henry reflects, "We never did get to cast a line from a bunk at that house, son, but we all cast other lines and hit something much better than what the waterways have to offer. Even better than Blackbeard's gold. Phil saved several lives. I married your mother and had a wonderful family. Billy married his sweetheart and did the same. He quit driving the gasoline truck and became a grocer. Jack was a successful structural engineer. He never forgot we should not have put the roof on first and gained a reputation for checking and rechecking his exemplary work. And Lafayette? He led men into battle in Korea, got a battlefield commission, and became a real gentleman, though he remained a rebel at heart.

"We went on with our lives and didn't do too bad for a bunch of shanty Irish. 'Bloom where you're planted,' the old Irish used to say. We kept the faith, loved our families, and cherished the memories, even the bad ones, and that half-built house at Tybee. The house was The Dorothy after all, certainly not The Margaret. Your mother never wavered, son, and stood fast until the end when I knew she saw the good Lord as she left us. May she rest in peace."

Phil listens from the driver's seat.

"That cast from the bunk is meaningless to me now, but those other things I talk about are priceless. Don't forget that, son. Please remember," Henry McGee exhorts his son.

"I will, Dad," Phil assures his father. "You taught us well, and so did Mom."

Henry McGee smiles, and a twinkle appears in his eyes, the "glint of Irish laughter."

"Let's go, Dad. Mom's in heaven, and so are all the others. Uncle Karl's son, Father Damien, will remember them at his Masses. I don't think he can bless houses that have disappeared in the wind, though," Phil says.

"Oh, we can bless all those things and thank God for them, son," the old man says. The Yuchi Indians used to say, 'All things are connected.' Right now, I'm connected with all those good things, especially your mother and our children and, of course, the Boys of the Summer of 1947. I love you, son, I love you all."

"I know you do, Dad, I know..." Phil responds.

The old man, who is past ninety now, slides his legs back into Phil's car and stares ahead with tears in his eyes. He smiles, shaking his head in wonderment at all that has transpired since those few months at Tybee so many years ago.

They drive back toward town. As they approach the Lazaretto Creek, Henry hears a familiar voice in his ear. It has been decades since he has heard it, but he recognizes it like it was yesterday. "You know what they call that bridge, Henry?"

"The Bridge to Everywhere, Phil," the old man answers in a whisper. "The Bridge to Everywhere."

THE END

Acknowledgments

From Father Tom Murphy

I'd like to express my gratitude to the following:

First and foremost, my parents, John Henry and Josephine Kenney Murphy (RIP), whose unwavering faith and perseverance have continuously inspired me.

To Fr. Mark Ross, whose encouragement ignited my passion for writing and whose belief in my work fueled my determination.

To Fr. Brett Brannen, Pastor of Saint Michaels Church on Tybee, for writing the Foreward to this novel and for your faithful friendship for over forty years.

I am deeply grateful to my sisters, Helen Marie Fleming, Mary Gene Sikes (my exceptional proofreader), Josie Murphy, and Michele Beckett, for their invaluable suggestions and contributions that shaped this book. A special thank you to my readers: Loretta Lominack, Fr. Gabe Cummings, Jack Krapf, Greg Jarres, Fr. Robert Chaney, my niece Maggie Thurber, and Tom McNamara. Their insightful feedback was instrumental in the editing process.

I would also like to remember Sister Georgette Cunniff (RIP), a dedicated Franciscan nun who staffed St. Michaels Catholic School on Tybee and shared stories of the Parish with me.

Finally, my deepest appreciation goes to Leigh Ebberwein,

Publisher, for her unwavering confidence in "The Bridge to Tybee" and her incredible patience during this endeavor.

Thank you all for believing in me and being part of this journey.

About the Author

THOMAS J. MURPHY, a native of Savannah, Georgia, has dedicated his life as a Catholic priest in the Diocese of Savannah for over 38 years. An alumnus of Armstrong State College and Mount Saint Mary's College and Seminary, he has a profound passion for serving his community. While his roots are firmly planted in Savannah, Fr. Tom has spent much of his ministry bringing faith and support to the small towns of South Georgia. Presently, he serves as a parish priest in Claxton, Georgia, where he is deeply inspired by the vibrant faith and warmth of the rural communities. Through his experiences, Fr. Tom shares a unique perspective on the beauty of small-town life and the bonds of faith that connect us all.

To learn more about Father Tom, visit his publisher's website Oldfortpress.com.